# The Best of Spicy Mystery

## Volume 3

# The Best of
# SPICY MYSTERY
## Volume 3

By

Hamlin Daly
Ellery Watson Calder
Carl Moore
Justin Case
E. Hoffmann Price
Robert Leslie Bellem

EDITED BY

Alfred Jan

BOSTON
ALTUS PRESS
2017

© 2017 Altus Press • First Edition—2017

PUBLISHING HISTORY

"Spicy Mysteries Re-Examined" Copyright © 2017 Alfred Jan.

"Medusa's Kiss" originally appeared in the January 1936 issue of *Spicy Mystery Stories*.

"The Strangler" originally appeared in the October 1936 issue of *Spicy Mystery Stories*.

"The Dark Veil" originally appeared in the June 1937 issue of *Spicy Mystery Stories*.

"Hands of the Dead" originally appeared in the June 1937 issue of *Spicy Mystery Stories*.

"Hearts From the Half Dead" originally appeared in the January 1937 issue of *Spicy Mystery Stories*.

"Hell's Dark Fragrance" originally appeared in the December 1936 issue of *Spicy Mystery Stories*.

"Thirst of the Damned" originally appeared in the March 1936 issue of *Spicy Mystery Stories*.

"Doom Door" originally appeared in the March 1936 issue of *Spicy Mystery Stories*.

"Dawn of Discord" originally appeared in the October 1940 issue of *Spicy Mystery Stories*.

"The Old Gods Eat" originally appeared in the February 1941 issue of *Spicy Mystery Stories*.

"Flowers of Desire" originally appeared in the September 1936 issue of *Spicy Mystery Stories*.

THANKS TO

Rebecca Burns, Alfred Jan and Chris Slembarski

# TABLE OF CONTENTS

# Alfred Jan

*T*HIS THIRD anthology is the result of my continuing efforts to find stories not following hackneyed weird menace plots. As mentioned in previous introductions, these predictable events include a man and a female companion finding themselves threatened by seemingly supernatural horrors only to find them to be human-caused after the villain is defeated and unmasked. The couple then emerges relieved and happy into the new dawn.

The assembled tales end with a twist, and not all end happily. For example, Ellery Watson Calder's carnivorous plants yarn ends unexpectedly as to the villain's identity. Colby Quinn's insane surgeon meets an unsatisfactory ironic end. Another Quinn contribution takes off on German Decadent horror master Hanns Heinz Ewers' classic "The Spider," a favorite of H.P. Lovecraft.

For fans of Robert Leslie Bellem and Clark Ashton Smith (one of the big three of *Weird Tales*, the others being H.P. Lovecraft and Robert E. Howard), I included some little known gems. One of the most prolific pulpsters, Bellem was not above recycling ideas. His "Flowers of Desire" in this book rehashes "Flowers of Enchantment" from the April 1928 issue of *Tales of Magic and Mystery*, concerning the fate of an archeologist obsessed with a strange woman he finds in a cave.

The Clark Ashton Smith completist should delight in two stories which he got discouraged with for some reason, and gave them to his friend and fellow pulp writer E. Hoffmann Price in 1939 to do whatever he wanted with them; he re-wrote them for

*Spicy Mystery.* "The Old Gods Eat"(1941), originally titled "The House of the Monoceras," tells of a cursed family's castle hiding a gigantic man-eating single-horned monster not explained away by natural means. In "Dawn of Discord" (1940), a scientist invents a machine to go back into human history, hoping to find the source of violence and extinguish it. Obviously he failed, but the story could be viewed as an anti-war statement published on the eve of World War II.

Works selected for these anthologies were mainly from the 1930s. While *Spicy Mystery* ended in December 1942, the early 1940s issues consisted mainly of reprints from the previous decade, published under various house names. The editors served time for these shenanigans in that they paid themselves instead of the real authors. Somehow, this adds to the disreputable mystique of the "Spicys" but does not detract from what I consider the best of *Spicy Mystery.*

*A practicing optometrist, Alfred Jan has edited short fiction collections by D.L. Champion (with Bill Blackbeard), Robert Leslie Bellem, and Joel Townsley Rogers, and contributed articles on Norbert Davis, Cornell Woolrich, and other pulp-related topics to* Blood 'N' Thunder *magazine. Alfred holds an M.A. in Philosophy, specializing in Aesthetics, and published freelance art criticism from 1982 to 1995. Work in progress includes a sample of works on ethics and aesthetics by the bohemian Gelett Burgess.*

HAMLIN DALY

# MEDUSA'S KISS

*One man succumbed to her beauty and died—was
it from fear? Another who loved her was found
"as though torn to pieces by a million barnacles!"*

*M*ILTON FROST, former shoe importer, had a
strong heart; so instead of taking a nose dive from a
penthouse parapet, like most ex-vice-presidents, he found himself
a job as a clerk in a Saint Augustine shoe shoppe.

As he swept out the shoppe, his dark, saturnine features looked
somewhat more grim than the ruins of Fort Matanzas. He was
wondering if he'd ever meet Quentin Harper, who had cleaned
the corporation out of everything but two cuspidors and a rose-
wood desk.

"I'll bite his liver out and spit it in his face, and then—"

But just then a customer entered. One glance, and Frost's
smile—not professional—made a fool of the Saint Augustine
sunshine. He forgot about Quentin Harper.

What the girl in the sunflower yellow ensemble planted on
the upholstery was something to dream about, and the silken
curves that flowed upward from her trim ankles as she put her
tiny hoofs on the foot rest would make anyone covet Frost's job.

Of course, taking her measure for tailor-made lingerie would
be even better, but then a fellow has to start at the bottom and
work his way up.

Her dark eyes were somewhat somber, but her face was as sweet
as the white roundnesses that would make her a million if she
ever tried posing for brassiere ads.

"Something for you, madam?"

"Don't call me madam, or I'll smack you!" she smiled. "Never

1

mind fondling the ankles. The shoes I want are for Mrs. Lambert, and I spend so much of my time saying 'yes, madam' to her it's a full-fledged gripe to hear the words between times—"

"If you really have any between times," suggested Frost, "I won't call you madam, not even in my sleep."

She eyed him a moment and seemed to like the lean, tanned, and somewhat angular features of a self-made man.

"That's almost a deal! But here's what I want—speaking of shoes again."

*SHE* handed him a list: a dozen pairs, everything from sports to evening models, in an odd size of an imported line the shoppe did not stock.

"Holy smoke, mad—er, darling!" he exclaimed.

"Diane," she corrected, "and hurry up with the shoes. Mrs. Lambert—"

The name was familiar.

"Irene Lambert?" he wondered. "Sorry, but I'll have to get them from Jacksonville."

"Irene is right, and she has a lovely grudge against anything connected with shoes, and she'll raise the roof. But how did you know her name?"

The absent customer must be one of the stockholders who had been crucified when his corporation was looted. He'd never met the lady. Which was lucky.

"Oh, nothing," evaded Frost. "But I'll get her the shoes."

"Right away?" She was eager.

"At thirty-five bucks a pair and business as it is, I'll say I can!"

And then he noticed that Mrs. Lambert's maid was wearing costly imported footgear: hand-me-downs, obviously, from her mistress. That was not odd, even though they were too new to be discarded in favor of the maid; but his expert eye saw that they were half a size smaller than the lot Diane had just ordered for Mrs. Lambert. And that was odd!

Why had Mrs. Lambert suddenly decided to get a complete change of footgear half a size *larger?*

*THE* manager enthusiastically approved of Frost's initiative, and sent him to Jacksonville.

Two hours later, Frost was on his way back, nosing his Ford down a dirt road that bypassed Saint Augustine. He presently saw that he had miscalculated: the narrow ribbon winding through luxuriant tropical vegetation might eventually lead to the Tocoi highway, but as a short cut it was the wrong number.

He throttled down to keep from capsizing. And forced to deliberation, his morning's fancies turned to selecting parking places in that tropical desolation where Diane wouldn't have to worry about passing traffic....

*"An O.D. blanket underneath the bough,"* he quoted, but before he completed his modernization of Omar, he saw that someone had beaten him to it—and with results that sent a blasting shiver through his veins.

Frost jammed the brakes.

A man lay huddled near the edge of a folded blanket spread on a hummock in the clearing not far from the road. There was something frozen about his stillness, something hideous about the clutching gesture of his right hand. Flies were swarming, but thus far no scavenging birds had arrived to complete the horror.

But as Frost approached he wished that the vultures had at least obliterated that man's face.

Frightened to death is a careless byword, but here it was a horribly apparent fact. He had jerked up to his knees, made a warding gesture, then toppled over—finished.

Despite the horror that branded that leaden mask, Frost saw that the victim had been one of those prosperous men whom the doctor advises to abstain from cigars, liquor, and highly seasoned meats—and who boldly insist they can take it. That is, until a shock proves the contrary.

No wounds, no signs of violence; not a trace of struggle. Just that ineradicable horror.

"If he'd had a better heart, he might still be running," decided Frost.

Then he checked his advance.

*IN* the soft, spongy ground were woman's shoe prints. Those leading to the blanket were close to the man's. They would be… but those leaving were wide spaced, heels barely registering.

Frost felt seasick, then felt as though he had thrust his hand into a basket of snakes; and when both sensations teamed up, he turned back to his car. As he took the wheel, he saw a heavy coupe a few yards ahead, parked on firm ground at the roadside.

He pulled up beside the abandoned car. Within he found a man's coat. The wallet contained several hundred dollars and a New York driver's license belonging to Clinton Hardy.

But what made the deepest impression on Frost was that the woman's footprints led toward the Tocoi highway. And they had been made by someone wearing an unusually small, *foreign last.*

You can't fool a veteran shoe man. French lasts are different; and American women don't like them until they get used to the difference.

Those prints had been made by a woman shod with imported footgear such as Diane had worn to town that morning. That thought kept him busy as he drove on.

*MRS. LAMBERT'S* bungalow was set well back on a crossroad intersecting the Tocoi highway. Across the way was another bungalow—vacant, judging from its surrounding tangle of rank foliage.

He parked, shouldered four hundred dollars' worth of shoes, and picked his way through the blaze of bignonias and hibiscus. The first jab at the doorbell brought Diane to the front.

She was not wearing her imported hand-me-downs.

Her eyes were wrathful until she recognized him smiling over a dozen shoe boxes.

"I'll see you before you leave," she whispered.

Then she led him to the left wing, tapped at a door, and announced, "The shoe salesman, madam."

A voice like night-blooming jasmine invited him in.

Irene Lambert's loveliness was shock number two for the day. Perhaps it was her amber-colored, unwinking eyes and slow, crimson smile: gold and red against incredibly white skin. Perhaps it was that undulant body enveloped—but not too much—by an apricot satin *peignoir*.

Having specialized in shoes, Frost did not know that Irene wore beneath the gown what the fashion experts called a four-gore combination in white crepe with dark lace; but he did know she had nice legs, languidly and invitingly stretched out on the ottoman at the foot of her chaise longue.

He wondered why she wasn't wearing mules. She hadn't kicked them off to make way for the shoe fitting. There weren't any in sight.

But that still did not explain Frost's distinct shock at getting his first eyeful of Irene Lambert's weird, eerie loveliness.

Perhaps it was her personality, which was about all that was entirely covered; though her breasts were veiled by the heaviest strands of the blackest hair he'd ever heard of.

What hair! Enough for several women. Her long fingers still curled about a great ivory comb, and as she greeted him, she still fondled that incredible, heavy cascade of blackness.

It wasn't silken hair. No silk could be that heavy. The strands were iridescent and clung to each other. They seemed to waver and writhe in the sunglow, as though endowed with separate life. Frost shivered.

Kneeling at the feet of beauty is natural for a shoe clerk. He hadn't expected her to be heated up by his touch—but neither had he anticipated the coolness of that chiffon-clad ankle.

"I'm sorry, Mrs. Lambert, but this shoe is… ah, about half a size too large," he announced. "Though it's exactly what you ordered—maybe I'd better—"

"They're perfect," she murmured. It sounded like the sigh of a tropical breeze. "Perfectly lovely…."

She leaned back among the cushions, picked up her long-handled mirror. Her arm was an ivory serpent, languidly grooming that iridescent hair.

The shoes were all the same last; but being handmade, Frost decided that each ought to be fitted.

And the pattern of the dark lace on that four-gore combination!

*He stared fascinated at her long and luminous hair, which seemed to live and glow in ropey strands, caressing her.*

If Frost ever took up needlework, he could duplicate it blindfolded....

But the study in lace was something to take in small doses. By the time the tourquoise and coral *lamé* evening slippers had been fitted, Frost was desperate.

**IRENE** smiled languorously over the mirror edge, and set it aside. Then a lingering, loving comb-touch, and she lifted that long hair clear of the hips it had been caressing.

Frost's head began swimming.

The damnable fascination of that woman! It wasn't that her topaz eyes had a come-on look. It was just the contrary. He was less than the furniture to her. Some chiffon had shifted, and she didn't even bother to pull it together....

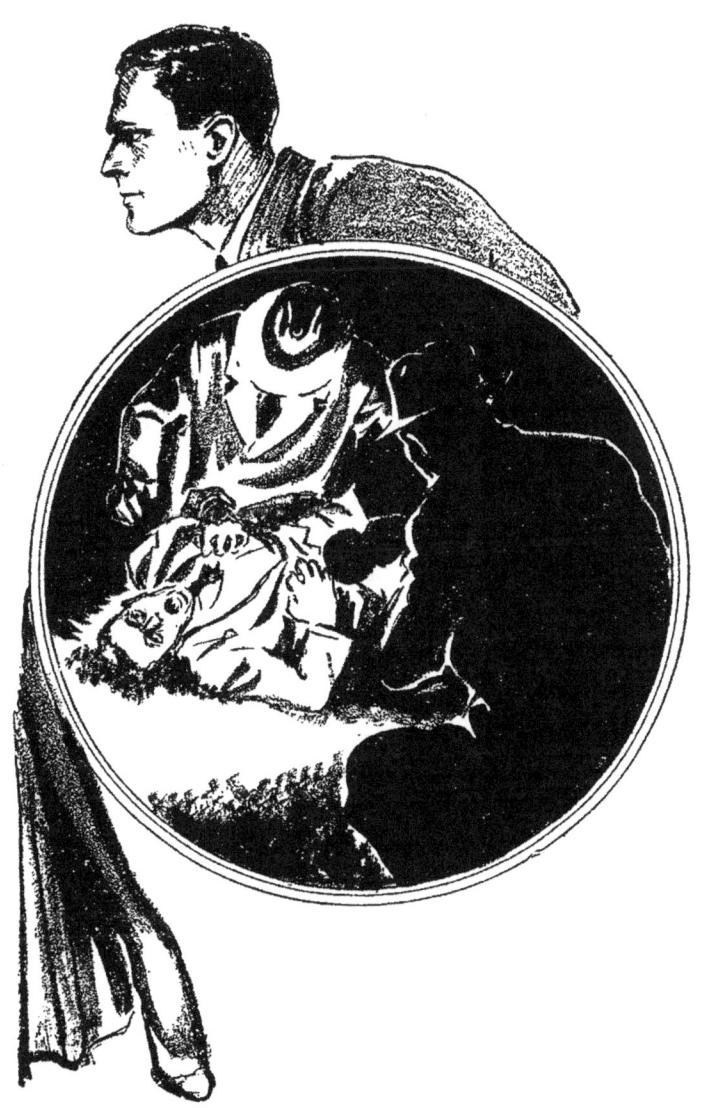

"My handbag is on the dresser… will you please get it?" she murmured.

He wondered why her white breasts rose and fell. Anyone so somnolent could scarcely be breathing. Yet somehow she seemed intensely alive.

He picked up the gold mesh bag. As he turned, his glance

caught an open wardrobe door. A heap of trees lay on the floor. The rack was empty.

Not a shoe in sight—except for the lot Frost had delivered.

A four hundred dollar customer is something to treasure. But Frost could stand just so much.

As he pocketed the bills she handed him, his free hand cupped flesh that had become unbearably fascinating. Despite the uncanny coolness, the contact thrilled him to desperation.

She did not cry out or slap him. Her smile was a languid riddle in crimson, and her eyes were mysterious pools of topaz.

An instant of blankness. He realized the enormity of his boldness. He was dazed by her utter calmness. She should have raised the roof—or liked it. They usually did the latter, with enough exceptions to lend interest.

But Irene Lambert's heartbeat was scarcely perceptible, and the imprisoned breast rose and fell in its unvarying, somnolent rhythm.

Frost sighed from his ankles.

If that was her way of asking for it—

Then he began getting familiar; but it did more to him than to that languid length of chiffon-shrouded ice.

He kissed her full on the lips, worked his way down that soft throat; and what his hands in the meanwhile learned about white crepe and dark lace was devastating.

Irene did finally stir, ever so languidly, and her smile was showing a trace of friendliness.

"You're awfully nice," she murmured.

She hitched herself back among the cushions.

Hopeful move! Now keep her with the right thought. Frost tried one that never failed.

But her arms did not close about him. She had picked up her comb and mirror.

"You won't mind, will you…."

There wasn't a bit of malice in her smile. Damn it, *she actually meant it!*

"Yeah... some other time," he croaked, swallowing his heart and licking dry lips.

*AT* the threshold he glanced back. For an instant he watched her combing that uncanny, iridescent hair. She had forgotten all about him.

Frost's ears felt like Mexican tamales when Diane met him at the back door. The hallway had been whirling too much for him to pick the front.

Diane curiously eyed him. She was wearing a neat blue house dress and a pair of cotton gloves. Smoke poured from the incinerator in the back yard.

"She is odd, isn't she?" Diane observed.

"Nuts!" growled Frost, feeling foolish.

Her next remark was made with her eyes: "How about that drive, some evening?"

"When?" he demanded.

"Tonight. She told me to check out and take in a show." Then, lowering her voice to a whisper, "I've got the key to that vacant bungalow, across the way. Wait, I'll get it for you."

Frost wondered at the fumes of burning leather issuing from the incinerator. One peep, and he understood Diane's stormy eyes.

It was stuffed with half consumed shoes. The last added was scarcely damaged: one of the pair Diane had worn that morning. Dog in the manger—though Frost used the feminine, being grammatically inclined—Irene didn't want the maid to wear her hand-me-downs.

Why not?

Frost fished it out of the incinerator and pocketed it. A hunch was growing.

Then Diane returned with the key.

"Come back tonight. Wait for me. I'll drive off in her car, park it somewhere nearby, and return."

Diane was worried plenty.

Frost's hunch took him past that sinister clearing just off the winding dirt road. He pulled up and applied the salvaged shoe to the footprints that led from what lay sweltering in the sun.

The fit was all too perfect.

Either Irene Lambert or her maid had fled from the terror that had walked by night.

By every rule, Frost should have reported his gruesome discovery to the police. But despite the destruction of the shoes—a more certain way of blocking investigation than having returned for the frisky business of eradicating footprints—something might yet involve Diane. And Frost wanted to question her in his own way.

*AND* that night he drove out to the Tocoi road, but not by any short cut! Even if a woman had escaped the swamp terror, Frost did not envy her.

He parked, then proceeded on foot to the vacant bungalow facing Irene Lambert's. There was a light in her window.

The latch yielded. He stepped into a musty darkness. The house was furnished. For half an hour he wafted, watching the brightness across the way.

Then Diane arrived.

"I'm awfully afraid," she whispered. "She's always been rather… well, odd. But burning those shoes, and nearly eating my head off for trying to snitch a pair—"

They picked their way through the gloom and found a lounge in the living room.

The routine that had left her mistress languidly indifferent soon had Diane clinging to him like a mechanic's lien.

Frost couldn't see whether she wore a four-gore combination or sackcloth, but that was no great loss. She was sweet and vibrant, and odd bits of obstructing lace heightened the suspense enough to make them both forget all about Irene Lambert's mania for destroying expensive shoes.

For a long time they forgot to whisper between kisses….

And then, as the rising moon began to invade the shadows, Diane began to get things off her chest—figuratively, of course.

"I've been with her for a couple of years," she said. "Ever since I had to scramble for a job. Awfully good to me, but she frightens

*That was odd! The shoes
she was ordering were
half a size too large!*

me half to death, sometimes... no, I don't have to comb her hair,
thank God!"

She shuddered, then added, "And she never goes to a hair-
dresser. It's a mania with her. It seems alive. Sometimes I think
it drinks up all her vitality."

Frost suppressed a heartfelt amen!

"And the worst of it is, she washes it in chicken blood—"

"*What?*"

"Yes. Chicken blood. Every week. That seems to pep her up a
lot. And makes it glisten with more colors than swamp water."

"Why not quit?"

"Oh.... I just can't. She's so terribly alone. Ever since that man
was found dead in her apartment, up north. Not long after she
lost so much money in the shoe company's stock."

*"Dead?* How—"

"Nobody knows. So utterly impossible that no human being could be suspected. They just marked it on the books. Irene came down here. Where she could be alone. Where the sun is warm. She loves it. Basks in that blistering blaze by the hour... like something dead."

"Where was she last night?"

"I don't know," answered Diane. "I was away. In her car. I think she had a heavy date. Which is unusual—"

*AND* then headlights blazed down the road. A heavy car crunched to a halt in front of the house across the street.

A man with a suitcase emerged. Frost sighed and relaxed, noting that he was lean and gaunt. He had no chance to see the stranger's face.

Diane's fingers sank into his arm.

"I thought so," she whispered. "That's why I've an evening off. Last night... and now tonight. And after all these months of seclusion... but maybe she's becoming human—"

"I doubt it!" Frost cut in.

The more he heard of Irene Lambert, the more he felt that he was on the verge of unpleasant revelations.

But Diane's warm curves snuggled closer....

Frost's consolation was terrifyingly interrupted.

The cry from across the street was a protest against outraged nature; but there was enough of lingering humanity about it to freeze Frost, make him think of that man who had died in the clearing. It was cut short. A strangled, gurgling gasp. Then it flared out again, a screech that ended in a horrible croaking.

And as Diane and Frost plunged into the hallway, they heard a splintering of glass, a sodden thud. Then a rustling in the foliage under Irene's shattered window.

"Oh, my God—did she—"

"That was a man—but maybe his yell drowned her voice—"

They cleared the gate. But as they bounded into the street, Frost saw four men breaking from cover and crashing through the yard toward Irene's door.

*For a moment her chiffon-clad loveliness halted them.*

A pounding. The blaze of flashlights. Then illumination from within. Irene Lambert was silhouetted against the hall light.

For a moment that chiffon-clad loveliness fascinated the four who halted at the threshold. Her hair streamed to her hips, gleamed with strange luminous lustre.

Frost seized Diane's hand; but before they could retreat, a flashlight beam picked them from the gloom.

"Steady!" barked a gruff voice. "The law."

A silver shield flashed, and light glinted from a blued pistol barrel.

Then, to Irene, "Is this the man?"

"Heavens, no!" purred that soft voice. "He jumped out the window."

Lights followed her gesture. And Frost, too shaken to protest about the grip still on his shoulder, accompanied the deputies.

But the hand dropped from him when they found what lay in the shrubbery. It still moved, but that would soon end.

What Frost had seen by the roadside that morning was sweetness and light compared to the excoriated mask that now stared up at him.

Horror beyond all mention blazed from those glassy eyes. The mere reflection of what that man had seen petrified Frost.

ONE of the deputies leaped forward, muttering; but before he could kneel to put a pistol to the ear of that now motionless thing, a companion restrained him.

Happily, the blood that oozed from every pore of that hideous mask blotted out the finer shades of terror. The man's shirt was drenched, and his tropical worsted trousers from belt to knees were a dripping, darkening sogginess.

"Give me that light!"

"All yours, Carson!" was the shuddering reply.

The sheriff knelt. Frost felt Diane's nails bite deeply into his wrist. She tried not to look, but nevertheless did.

Trembling hands tore open the sodden shirt Chest, like face, was riddled by uncounted tiny holes from which blood no longer dripped.

A six-fold sigh from the group. It was dead.

"Like a man torn all to pieces on a million barnacles," muttered the sheriff. "Only no barnacles ever made a clean sweep like this.... God...."

They turned to Irene Lambert. A hoarse question; but instead of answering, she beckoned to the door.

Once inside, she explained, "Honestly, I don't know how it

happened, sheriff. We were sitting here. I was rather nervous, trying to kill time until you arrived to arrest him—"

"I know all that!" rasped the sheriff. "But what chewed him up?"

Frost, watching that languid smile and those topaz eyes, began to understand: Irene had trapped someone wanted by the police.

"Really, sheriff... it all happened so quickly. We'd had a few words. I think he must have suspected the trick. He snatched his suitcase, pushed me to one side—"

Her hand crept upward to indicate the perceptible bruise at the base of her throat.

"But the suitcase? Where?"

She pointed into the corner, and continued, "But he suddenly cried out terribly, and jumped through the window."

It was shattered. But no window pane had ever left a million tiny punctures in anyone's skin.

Frost saw the scattered contents of the walrus hide bag.

Bonds... reams of bearer bonds... loot into the hundreds of thousands. Then he saw the initials: *Q.H.* That was a jolt! Quentin Harper! The man who had brought about his own financial downfall!

"But Harper wouldn't have shrieked that way just because he thought the law was waiting. And he'd have run to the rear."

*IRENE* was perplexed. Having made her statement, she stepped back a pace, plucked a comb from her dresser, and abstractedly groomed that shimmering length of heavy blackness trailing past her hips. But Frost's mind was still on his old enemy.

Q.H.—Quentin Harper, the slick article whose manipulations and embezzlements had left Frost holding the bag! He had evaded the law only to be tricked into a fatal rendezvous by this languid siren.

"How did you ever meet him, Mrs. Lambert?" This from the sheriff.

"Half my investments were wiped out by his thievery," she softly answered. "So I waited. Crooks like to hide in Florida. And I was right—"

Her candor was amazing. But it could be: for neither human nor animal could in an instant thus riddle a man.

The law left with the remains. Another case to decorate the books. Frost's story, modified to eliminate Diane's meeting him in the bungalow, had closed the inquiry. He had seen nothing to account for the attack.

But Frost knew that there was in the expression of the man in the swamp something akin to what branded Quentin Harper's face.

Irene Lambert turned to Frost.

"You've been very kind," she murmured. Then she turned to her maid: "Please run to the village and get some brandy. I feel… well, a bit shaken."

She said it in such a way that Frost could not himself volunteer to accept the errand.

Diane's "*Yes, madam,*" clinched it. Frost's interposition would have been a dead giveaway. She was not afraid to drive alone, and she was glad that he had not openly linked himself with her.

Irene listened to the whirr of a starter. Then as a motor purred out the drive, she stretched herself on the chaise longue and beckoned to Frost to seat himself at the foot.

"Your story about coming back with a pair of shoes was quick-witted," she began. "And saying that there just was a scream and a crash of glass—well, that made my incredible story convincing.

"But I want you to tell me the truth. Before Diane returns."

"*What did happen?* I was so—dazed—"

And that stopped Frost. She actually meant the question.

**SHE** was genuine. Baffling, but genuine as her hair combing that afternoon. He hesitated.

She misunderstood his silence and leaned forward.

"Please tell me." No mistaking the pleading note, nor the bewilderment in her eyes.

His glance shifted from her iridescent black hair and down that white body not quite hidden by satin and crepe.

"I'm sorry about this morning," she murmured. "I didn't mean to hurt your feelings… but I simply can't pretend."

Damn it, she was human! She had misunderstood his silence. No cunning woman would possibly offer such a remark to smooth over the sting of their first meeting.

"I'm dreadfully afraid," she resumed. "Things like… like what happened… have happened before. And this is the first time there's been a witness—don't try to be tactful about Diane—I know you were with her—"

The crimson smile was friendly and reassuring. And that smooth, cool body was swaying forward and up from its supporting cushions.

"I was dreadfully worried, this morning, wondering whether that crook would take the bait…."

Naively tactless apology for hair combing! She couldn't have any subtle trick up her sleeve. Not after such a boner! She was as much as telling him that she'd not reach for her comb now. But he wasn't sure he penetrated all the significance of her remarks.

The fascination that had led Frost to foolhardy familiarity was again moving him. The beating of his heart now made his ears ring and rumble… it must be a strong heart to stand such an overload.

The desire for her inviting body now stirred more than his own flesh; it was burning intolerably into his very soul. High-breasted, white seductiveness that flattened into whiter sleekness—

No matter how cold she might be, the sheer perfection of her was maddening.

He found her lips, cool and questing as the arms that slid about him like ivory serpents. He felt her sigh and tremble, saw her eyelids drop long lashes over those topaz eyes… and that in itself was a wonder. He'd doubted that those unwavering eyes had lids.

The rippling, suave coolness of her was becoming an exquisite torment….

"You'll tell me, later, won't you?" she whispered.

*A SOUL-BURNING* embrace seized every fibre of his body. For a moment he was dizzied and scarcely realized what was happening; but when he finally knew, there followed an

*"Oh God, what'll we do?" moaned Diane. "I killed her!"*

everlasting age in which he could not move, could not even believe his knowledge.

Her hair was flowing in great rippling strands over his shoulders, twining lovingly about his throat, creeping—creeping like uncounted living serpents to his waist. Uncounted tiny tongues were sifting through his shirt, caressing his flesh.

A tangle of long, hairlike serpents drew him closer to her hungry mouth and trembling body. That flowing hair had crept from beneath her and was now a living canopy of innumerable clinging strands.

He knew now that terror had killed Irene's lover by the roadside. He knew now that wrathful serpents had excoriated her enemy, Quentin Harper. And though they were caressing him, horror forced a throat rending cry from his lips.

Frost had a strong heart. So he lived to tear away from those murmuring crimson lips and through that all-possessing, serpentine hair. He was not clear of her accursed caress, but his head was above the enfolding nightmare.

Her arms followed him, and her eyes opened in bewilderment, in uncomprehending dismay.

He cried out again, fiercely jerked back. A heart has its limits.

And then there was a shrill scream and a flash before his eyes. The clinging serpents suddenly relaxed. Off balance, he crashed to the floor; but even as he fell, there was another shriek: an outcry that penetrated even into his blinding horror and forced him to look.

Irene was writhing on the chaise longue, clutching the severed ends of her hair. Diane, paper white, was behind her. In her hand was a gardner's sickle—a steel crescent, now dripping hideously. And the heavy strands that dropped from Frost's body also dripped.

FRENZY drove them into the night; but as they fled, Frost saw that Irene Lambert was now still as her severed hair. He knew now that those heavy tresses had been washed in chicken blood so that they would not drink all her own; that her hair was a living part of her—serpent and woman!

"Oh, good God... what'll we do... I killed her," moaned Diane. "I was afraid, so I didn't go to the village."

"No one will believe the truth," was Frost's trembling reply. "How could a haircut be fatal?"

Then, as Diane pondered on his proposed answer to the law, he added, "She wasn't trying to hurt me. But you didn't know that Medusa could have her affectionate moments...."

*"Medusa?"*

"Yes. The snake-haired woman whose glance turned people to stone. Like many other antique myths, that one seems to have its foundation. No legend is ever made up entirely of fancy.

"There must have been, uncounted centuries ago, a race of serpent-haired people. And Irene's an atavism. A throwback to something that lived ages past, when all creation was reptilian. There are such things. More than the public ever suspects.

"She probably never fully realized how her serpents took possession of her consciousness. A flare of rage—and Quentin Harper was finished, much to her perplexity a moment later when her human side returned."

He added a few words about the horror in the swamp, then concluded, "And her affection frightened *him* to death. Then, only half sensing how it had happened, she fled. But something prompted her to destroy her shoes just in case there was an investigation."

The dripping sickle dropped from Diane's fingers.

"Medusa," she murmured as comprehension sank home. "Thank God I returned!"

But as they drove to the city, Frost cursed that curved blade. It had robbed him of something a strong heart might have endured... something that no man had known for uncounted millions of years....

# THE STRANGLER

*She was a lovely young widow, but Rad
couldn't forget that both her husbands had
hanged themselves. And to learn what fatal
spell this woman cast upon the men who
loved her—Rad became one of them!*

**T**HERE WAS no question of murder in the coroner's mind; the girl's husband had simply hanged himself to a ceiling fixture. Nothing too odd about that, Rad Mason admitted; people did it every day.

No, it wasn't any notion of a scoop that made him follow the girl from the inquest room: he had just remembered—and he wondered if any other reporter had—that about two years ago, this woman had had another husband. He, too, had hanged himself.

So it was just curiosity; or maybe that wasn't the word for the quickening of the pulse he had felt after watching her steadily.

At the sidewalk she found him at her elbow. "Let me see you home?" he asked. "I'm a reporter, but I promise not to bother you." While he spoke, his eyes were on the silk red scarf wound high around her throat; funny thing to wear with a black dress—or was she supposed to be in mourning?

"Thanks." She let him help her into a cab and sat very close to him as they started off.

Rad felt dizzy now, as though he'd been drinking; and his heart contracted as the girl's fingers, warm and sinuous, caressed the thick biceps of his upper arm.

But still, looking down at her, the chief thing he noticed was not her beauty or the slinky figure denying her dress with every sensuous curve: what caught his eye was the red scarf, full and closely tied as though she considered her throat an intimate part of her, to be covered from masculine eyes. A quick ache swelled

21

in his own throat, and Rad wanted to tear away the scarf and touch the white skin beneath. He swallowed hard.

"What's your name?"

"Ariadne." Her smouldering eyes caressed him. Then she said simply, "I like a man to be big and husky." She hugged herself closer, and his blood beat high at the touch of her little breast against his elbow.

(What was her nationality, anyway, Rad wondered? Dark, olive-skinned, she might have been a Greek....)

He felt guilty for her: her husband had died today, and already she made up to another man. He felt ashamed too because he invited it; because he was meeting her half way. Even if she could forget, he couldn't put out of his mind that her last lover had just died... and violently!

**INSIDE** her rooms, Rad caught an instant shock of surprise; for although it was an ordinary brownstone house, these rooms smelled of must and age... of dankness and dust and cobwebs.

Cobwebs. The first thing Rad saw, in fact, was a cobweb in one corner of the living room, near the ceiling. There was a gleam of

movement, a scuttling small thing, and Rad rushed over to kill
the spider.

"No!" Ariadne caught his arm frenziedly. "Don't, please—she's
my pet." Then, as if she sensed the cold shiver that iced down his
spine; "But seriously, be careful—it's bad luck to kill a spider, you
know."

She was smiling, but the smile was set, and her eyes were
narrow, and her fingers were like prongs of steel gripping his arm.

Rad shrugged, wiped a bead of sweat from his forehead. Then he grinned. "A spider's only a spider," he told her. "But somehow, this one gives me the creeps."

He stared up at the motionless insect. It was about an inch long, and the surface of its yellow-spotted black body seemed to be smooth and silky rather than hairy; and around the foremost of the two divisions of the body was a thin scarlet band. The creature's crouching legs moved, the web shook, and Rad looked away.

"Why," he asked casually, "did you say she?"

Ariadne's black eyes were amused. "Can't you tell a female spider? They're larger. I've seen her trap the males; she always kills them, sucks them dry."

"Well, for God's sake, let's talk of something else!"

He turned, found himself close against her; and instantly they forgot the spider. The girl's eyes were shining, she was smiling, and she tore off his coat and shirt so that she could see his big muscles, his deep chest; and she trembled as she ran her fingers over the thick hair of his forearms.

Rad put his hands in the middle of her back and forced her close against him, and she fought a little—as if she liked to be forced. Her breast heaved sharply to fast breathing; her low-lidded eyes were black and scintillant with excitement. Her soft lips were wet and very red, and when they began twitching and exposed the edges of her sharp little teeth, Rad started—it looked almost like a snarl....

She buried her lips against his shoulder and he shivered as he felt her teeth touching his skin like warm needles.

"Here!" he muttered huskily. He forced her chin up and kissed her mouth; he lifted her and she clung to him as if wild, her body a live thing of liquid undulance, her breast sliding against his chest as he drew her up; and the toes of her shoes struck him viciously as they dangled a foot above the floor.

Rad sat down with her on a couch, and he fondled the edge of the red scarf with eager fingers, not knowing what there was about it that attracted him so.

"*No!*" the girl's eyes widened and she tore her lips from his mouth. "No, no!" she gasped. "*Not… yet!*"

She pulled his fingers from the scarf and held them in her own warm hand. Rad could feel her heart beating like the throb of a struggling bird's wings, and he knew she was finding it hard to breathe.

Suddenly her face darkened to a surge of blood; she pulled her mouth away and gulped in air as if she felt strangled.

"I feel faint." She put her head down against her knees. Somehow she had kicked off her shoes, and Rad could see her toes curling through thin chiffon.

*WHEN* she sat up again, she loosed the knot of hair at the nape of her neck and let it fall in a shower down her back. And though she lay as if exhausted in his arms, Rad felt her heart pounding harder than ever; felt the fits of trembling that broke over her in shocks.

She asked in a voice so calm it startled him:

"Did you ever hear of a woman choked with her own hair? Look!" And she wound her hair into a rope and looped it around her neck, over the scarf, and pulled hard with both hands.

Rad swallowed with difficulty. Her eyes were now wide and gleamed terribly at him; her face became suffused with blood and her lips fell apart and faded from red to a full blue.

At that instant she held her mouth close to his and he felt himself kissing her almost against his will. The feel of lips so firm and turgid with blood inflamed his senses; his kiss was savage and mashing.

Then—she had let go her hair and was smiling at him hungrily as her face regained its natural color. She slid from his lap; stood up and tugged at the shoulder snaps of her dress.

The black garment fell away and he saw her in brief step-ins and lace brassiere and sheer dark cobwebby stockings reaching far up her lovely thighs.

One other thing she wore: the red scarf.

But, when Rad seized her and held her against her struggles; when he held the writhing warm length of her against him and kissed her, she worked her hands free, untied the knot, and tore the red scarf away.

There were dark, yellowish-blue bruises on her throat.

She caught his hands and carried them to her throat.

"Choke me… choke me!" she moaned.

In a horror at himself, Rad felt his shaking fingers clutch her slender throat, sink cruelly into the hot pliant flesh… felt his mighty thumbs block the hammering pulse at each side of her jugular. In a horror because, while he wanted this girl with a violence he had never experienced before, yet repugnance gripped him at the very thought of harming her, of bruising the tender skin that he wanted to kiss instead. Yet—he wanted her… enough to do anything she asked.

Through a reddening haze he saw her face grow darker and darker with blood; watched with curious detached repulsion while her eyes bulged; hating himself for it all, yet induced, hypnotized by the loveliness he hoped would be his reward.

Then he kissed her, and the contact of her lips, hot and slick with the moisture of her blood-thickened tongue, nearly drove him mad.

Suddenly she slumped, and he thought she was unconscious and he released her throat, instantly contrite for his unwonted brutality. But the faint gasp of her voice pierced the rhythmic drumming in his ears. "More! More…!"

He shuddered. How could he—? But his huge hands closed again and he felt her arms around him, hugging her body against him as closely as she could. She must have bitten her own tongue, for her kiss was wet and salty to his taste, and a thin stream trickled down her chin.

And as he kissed her, he felt his lips twitching and lifting from his teeth. Ariadne was struggling, yet at the same time hugging herself to him so furiously that he thought she must have more than one pair of arms. He thought of the multiple arms of the female spider.… Then he seemed to be floating with her down, down into a feathery softness of untasted ecstasy.…

When Rad left her and stole out of the house, it was dark, and he looked about him furtively and slunk like a wolf in the shadows.

*Down, down she plunged, the red scarf streaming.*

$NEXT$ morning he fled for refuge to Ellen Gar, the girl he planned some day to marry; and now he felt more himself. Kissing this girl, feeling a fresh innocence about her, he could look back on last night as upon a nightmare. He wanted to tear from his memory the savage caress of that other girl; that darkly lovely one he had left barely conscious from the brutality she had drawn out of him.

Suddenly he drew back from Ellen, shaken.

"Rad!" she cried. "What is it? You look like—like a ghost!"

Rad didn't feel like a ghost. He had caught himself toying with her hair, running his fingers tentatively over the soft skin of her throat. Had the embrace of Ariadne made a beast of him?

For three days Rad didn't trust himself to go near Ellen. And in these three days he fought the temptation, crawling like an itch in him, to go again to Ariadne's rooms. He could still remember her as he'd last seen her in the half darkness, moaning in ecstasy and holding her bruised throat with her hands, unable to answer his goodbye as he turned fearfully toward the door, shying a little to one side as he remembered the she-spider crouched there in her web.

He wasn't sure Ariadne had been fully conscious when he left her, but he'd sworn not to go back.

On the fourth day, just after dark, she was letting him into the musty-smelling room; she was smiling at him and he was already catching his breath at the way her beauty, the lovely curves and contours of her body, was revealed by the thin negligee... catching his breath, too, and feeling his hands start trembling, when he saw the red silk scarf wound high under her chin.

She caught his hands in hers and pulled him from the door. "You ran away," she accused. But then she laughed as if humoring him. "But I couldn't blame you; my wild way of making love must have—frightened you."

Rad felt himself blushing as he put his arms around her. "Would I be back," he forced himself to say, "if I wasn't still nuts about you?"

She laid her cheek against his heart and said softly: "But I'm not excusing myself.... I'm just—well, very feminine—that way: I like to be handled rough by a big strong man. And you're the—" she shivered in his arms—"you know how I feel about you by now!"

*RAD* felt the fire mounting in his blood again. In the back of his mind was the thought that the caveman stuff she liked was a little stronger than any he'd ever run up against, rougher than the way *he* enjoyed treating a girl—but he didn't voice it.

Looking over her head, he saw a movement in the corner high on the wall and muttered:

"That damned spider's still here."

"I told you," she laughed, "that she's my pet. Forget the thing and come kiss me…."

He kissed her while he lifted her slim and light body; felt, through the gauzy stuff of her negligee, flesh of her, firm and warm against his forearm. His arm slid up under her knees and the fine grain of her stockings was tight-stretched against his wrist.

He sat down with her and kissed her closed eyes; his pulse beat faster because he knew within him what was going to happen. His lips seemed magnetized as he kissed her; against his own will he kept nibbling playfully at the edge of the red scarf, and after a few minutes, when she slowly untied and removed the scarf, Rad felt almost as if he were being choked himself, it was so hard to breathe. He knew what she expected of him as plainly as if she had spoken.

He closed his muscular fingers about her defenseless throat and kissed her while he choked her. In a minute she tried to break away, but Rad was seized by an impulse to squeeze until her neck broke. It wasn't an idea of pleasure, but of self-preservation: the instinct of man to destroy his natural enemy. It was the same impulse that had seized him from the very first day—*to crush the spider!*

For a single murderous moment, he only laughed into her lips at the desperate way she struggled and kicked against him, weaker and weaker….

But finally he let her go, aghast that he had thought of killing the girl he wanted more than anything in the world.

When she got her breath back, she looked up at him. "Damn you!" she whispered fiercely, and her eyes blazed. "I love you! I love you!"

Then from the couch behind her she brought a length of thin

She stood before him lovely and alluring, but he couldn't forget that accursed spider—the loathesome insect she had said was her pet.

strong cord, black and fine of weave and silky, like her hair. It was about five feet long.

"Here." She doubled the cord and placed it in his hand.

"What the hell—"

Ariadne stood up from his lap shrugged off the negligee and stood with her back to him. His eyes dropped from her brassiere strap to the thin lacy step-ins snugged about the warm curves of her hips.

Now she held her hands behind her.

"Tie my hands," she commanded. "Tight, so I can't get away."

Hungry for her embrace, for her lips, Rad started to object. Then he shrugged. He wound the cord tightly round her wrists and tied her. His heart was throbbing in his throat.

He whirled her about roughly, crushed her in his arms; and she smiled and looked at him with narrow-slitted eyes.

"I love you more," she explained softly, "when I feel so helpless."

To feel helpless, she knew still another trick: she held herself absolutely passive and unresponsive to his caresses for a long time.

Suddenly she said, "Untie me now."

"Hell no!" Rad laughed grimly. "I like you this way."

Again he was seized with that deadly premonition that it would be better for him if he would choke her, not playfully, not to humor her and win her favor, but in earnest—to the finish.

"Damn you! Un—" But he choked off her words and her breath and when finally the red haze cleared from his eyes and he released her throat, she was gasping and sobbing and kissing him at the same time.

"Untie me," she pleaded. "The spider—I want you to see something."

*RAD* untied her with a sinking, uneasy sensation. She led him to the corner and showed him the female spider winding her web around a helpless black male. They watched, the girl with quickening breath and Rad with revulsion, while the yellow-spotted black one, with the scarlet band around her, first embraced and then killed the prisoner, sucking the life fluid away until his body was only a drained and withered husk.

Rad pulled Ariadne away. "Why the hell do you like to watch that?" he asked, disgust in his voice.

She smiled and kissed him. "Don't be angry. I just like to see the female besting the male. With me, it's the other way around; see how *you* manhandle me and knock me around and choke me half to death, darling? While you—you're so strong I couldn't ever hurt you."

Laughing, with a playful gesture, she looped the silk cord over his head and pulled it tight under one ear. Rad grinned and tensed the thick, corded muscles of his neck.

"Pull," he invited.

She pulled on the cord with all her strength, but couldn't budge the muscles guarding his windpipe. He breathed easily.

But then he realized something. The cord was blocking the veins next to the surface of his skin, while the arteries still carried blood to his head... and his face was becoming turgid with the blood dammed there. He felt somewhat as if he were going under an anesthetic; his thought came slowly; he grew a little dizzy and leaned his lips against Ariadne's, felt her sharp little teeth touch his lower lip. But instead of taking the cord away, she pulled the harder.

And Rad, his sight a little blurred, carried away by the girl's own frenzy, felt a desire to let her have her way for a few moments; he had shown that she couldn't hurt him; he could of course break away any time he wished.... He relaxed his neck muscles and the cord bit deeper. His tongue swelled; his sight grew red; and pressure began to pulse and hum against his eyeballs.

It was about time, Rad thought lazily, that he took another deep breath, but he didn't quite know how to tell her to take the cord away. He lifted his hands to her wrists, but she kissed him softly and he dropped his hands again. He wanted only for her to keep on kissing him. And then—he was kissing her and time seemed to stand still and hum just above his head like a huge turbine spinning at intense speed; spinning, spinning....

**SUDDENLY** the spinning stopped with a jerk and he found himself choking while she held him in her arms on the floor.

"What the devil—!" he groaned, his voice raw and raspy. "You trying to kill me?"

She laughed and then murmured consolingly in his ear: "But I thought you liked it."

Ice laid itself around his heart. Liked it—hell! Couldn't she tell that he was only doing all this to please her? But of course not—if she had thought he was merely playing up to her to win her, she'd throw him down.

Rad left her a few minutes later and his spirit lifted at the thought of sunshine. Out in the open air he was more able to think; he could see more clearly what a damned fool he had been. Why, that girl was a witch! A sort of hypnotist; a drug that worked on a man and might.... Well—there! he almost had it. There was a good story here somewhere: why had this girl's two husbands hanged themselves? Wasn't there a hint in the way he'd just a moment ago remained passive while she slipped a cord about his neck and choked him unconscious. Had she actually hanged these men? No... a girl couldn't have done it. But....

*RAD* stayed away two days this time, and professional jealousy drove him back: a brief article hidden in the middle pages of a Sunday feature section of a tabloid. There weren't more than two hundred words about Ariadne:

> *"... lovely young widow... has been married twice, and each time, after a few weeks, her husband committed suicide by hanging himself. Is she a jinx? What fatal spell does this woman cast upon the men who love her?"*

More stuff like that. Rad folded the paper into his pocket and swung out of the office. But as be started to give the cab driver Ariadne's address, a pang shot through him and his neck began to itch where the silk cord had bitten in.... An intense prescience of tragedy filled him and then was gone in a second.

He gave the driver his sweetheart's address. He'd tell Ellen something about the case; leaving out the facts, he could tell her where he was going—tell her he was working on a good story. Something told him he ought to let the police in on it at this stage. But what could they arrest Ariadne for except being a little insane?

The real reason he didn't want to tell anyone about her, Rad realized, was that he wanted her to himself; she was like a drug— he had to have her!

So he didn't tell Ellen after all. He kissed her lightly, mumbled excuses for not having been to see her, and absent-mindedly made a date. He wanted to leave now; his mind was in a fever thinking of Ariadne. Then Rad came to with a shock and realized that Ellen was staring intently at his neck: she had seen the line of bruise stretching around his neck where the cord had tortured his flesh.

"What's that?" she asked sharply.

"Nothing." Rad turned up his collar; he'd kept it turned up in the office and had kept his chin down. "Nothing at all."

He walked out without explaining. He had to shove her back inside and shut the door.

Cursing himself, he rushed into the cab and sailed toward Ariadne's.

*SHE* was desperately glad to see him; he could tell that. But she was sore, too, because he had stayed away for two days.

Rad didn't look for the spider this time; he drew out the newspaper and showed her the article.

"Did you ever hear of anything sillier," Rad asked, watching her narrowly. "It's a shame they write stuff like this about you."

Her eyes were dark and sad, her gaze level into his. "Maybe," she said, "I am a jinx. Maybe you'd better stay away from me."

"What rot!" Rad exclaimed.

He dropped the paper and they were in each other's arms in an instant. He untied the red scarf and kissed the discolored smooth skin of her throat She jerked back at the touch of his lips, as though the bruises were hypersensitive; but then she yielded and pressed herself upon him, moaning with delight as his mouth traversed the places under her jaw and chin and ear.

When she brought out the doubled black cord, Rad caught a deep breath and couldn't let it out for an instant. Without touching him or saying anything, she looked into his eyes for a long moment, and Rad reached trembling hands for the cord, without his own will's bidding.

But instead of tying her hands, he wound the cord around his own neck and gave her the ends. He felt his soul freeze as he realized in a subconscious way what he was doing. The cord tightened as he pressed her slim body close; and as he thrilled to the trembling soft warmth of her, as he kissed her hungrily, he braced himself against the ring of pain that cut in and downward… and then he yielded. He knew now that to hold this lovely creature in his arms he could suffer anything—even the sensation of tortured laceration of his throat, the agony of having his breath blocked and withheld from his lungs while he rained furious kisses on her and crushed her in a tighter embrace.

Things revolved in a black cloud, and when he again saw her clearly, she was holding his head against her breast on the couch and murmuring into his hair. He looked up, and her eyes were terribly bright and shiny—yet deep: like two black worlds into whose luring depths he ached to be drawn.

She was kissing him then, and letting him drink his fill of the message in her eyes, and making love to him so ardently that he didn't realize that he had the black cord in his hand. Her lips were moving, and when he realized the import of what he was saying, horror filled him, invaded him like a sweet drugged wine…. For of course she was right: what she was suggesting was just what he had been going to do all the time!… was just what he had known that he would do!

She was telling him softly, persuasively, that he must come with her and look at the spider; must climb up and observe the ominous web that housed her little pet. And the vision of that loathsome web filled him with terror… yet he couldn't help himself—he must do what she wished—anything to please her, to hold her in his arms forever!

*THEY* had walked together to the corner of the room and he found that he couldn't reach the spider's web. So Ariadne brought a chair. And when he climbed up, the web and the motionless spider with its beady eyes drew him like a hypnotic lure; so that he hardly realized that Ariadne had noosed the cord about his neck, that she was beside him on the chair, looping the cord over a thick hook near the web. For a moment she hugged herself to him and pressed the soft mounds of her breasts against him and kissed him—and he seemed to be seeing more and more deeply into the black worlds of Ariadne's eyes. Then she was gone. He drew a full breath and gazed at the spider, and agony enveloped him in a blinding sheet. Ariadne had jerked the chair from under him. Pain radiated down from the fiery ring of rope and was forgotten.

For now his head was swelling... expanding to a bubble with the lightness of air. And he was suspended blissfully in the frothy atmosphere; breathing air as sharply pungent as ether; and holding Ariadne in his arms and kissing her... kissing her....

And that kiss, he felt, was causing him to open his mouth; his tongue was swelling outward between tortured lips. Now the bliss was receding and he knew only waves of pain pounding his head with every blow of his laboring heart.

*And he knew—he knew!—that the black spider was crawling over his face!*

He couldn't feel, but somehow he knew that the yellow-spotted she-spider was crawling, crawling, pushing with its eight horrible long legs; surely approaching his mouth.

A swift vision of the black male spider, defeated and torn; betrayed and drained of life while in the trap of passion. Soon, now, the head of the female spider, with its encircling scarlet band, would touch his lips; the thin black legs would crawl over his tongue.... God! Where was Ariadne? Wouldn't she help him?

But now, with terrifying abruptness, black fog squeezed over his consciousness. Rad tried to grit his teeth and hold out....

"*RAD!* Rad!" Ellen Gar's blonde head was bent close to his face when he opened his bloodshot eyes. Rad even recognized the two police detectives with her.

All Rad could say was, "What the hell—!" At least he thought he could say that, but he only croaked.

They trickled water between his lips, and one of the detectives lifted something from the corner of his mouth. Rad saw that it was the severed leg of a spider.

He muttered a hoarse curse and groaned, with head in his hands.

"I followed you," Ellen said. "You acted so—queer. I thought you were crazy. Of course I didn't want to spoil your story, but when we heard thumps—it must have been your feet kicking the wall—we busted in. Rad, who did it?"

"Did you see anyone else?" he asked swiftly.

"No."

"Well…." How could he explain, now? Horrifying as the story was to him, it wouldn't sound reasonable to them. He finally told them about the girl; said she had drugged him and then hanged him. "It's the same one whose husbands always hang themselves," he added before they had time to wonder how a girl could hang his two hundred pounds to a wall hook.

"We'll find that girl," one of the detectives swore.

Rad looked at the spider web. Strangely, it hadn't been destroyed. But beside him lay the body of the female spider, mangled where he had crushed it by closing his mouth. One leg was missing; he didn't see it just now.

But Rad stared at the body of the spider and did not think they would find Ariadne.

"Funny there's no furniture here," one of the men said. "Nothing but that old chair."

Rad stared in amazement. There was no couch, no bed, no sign of habitation.

*THEY* did find Ariadne. They told Rad that she had jumped or fallen from the bathroom window, for her body—with a red scarf around her throat—was found directly below in a narrow alleyway. They even explained how one arm had been almost torn off by the slicing impact of a corrugated iron fence.

Rad shuddered. Remembering the spider's leg that had been lifted from his lip, he returned to the room to look again at the insect's body.

But the dead spider was gone. Nothing remained now but the web; tenuous, bleak, deserted. The two detectives and Ellen denied having touched the thing; but they didn't see what difference it made, anyway.

"And listen," one of the dicks told him, "this tale about a girl having this apartment… the landlord says it's been empty for weeks."

# ChE DARK VEIL

*When two girls loved him, Ross put his fame
as a surgeon first… only to find he had
disturbed occult forces of hate and passion that
were greater than his skill with the knife*

*IN SUGGESTING* the operation, Dr. Nathan Ross was thinking of love; of the satisfaction and pleasure of winning the one of the two girls he really cared for. But he was thinking also of his professional reputation; of the write-ups, the fame, that would build around his name if he succeeded in separating Siamese twins.

He stopped pacing and looked down at the two girls reclining tensely in the leather divan of his home office.

"Of course, I love you," he said smoothly, speaking to neither in particular. "But I can't marry both of you! I can't even marry one of you, in fact; because you couldn't get a license to marry in this state—or any other state that I know of."

They sat side by side, joined at the hips by a narrow formation of bone. The Castle twins. They were lovely; they were young; and they both loved him.

Ross sat down beside them He took each young figure in his arms in turn; kissed red lips: Mary's—whom he loved; Peg's—for whom he felt an instinctive distrust mingled with an attraction that he denied to himself.

He leaned back, shrugged. "So you see how it is. It sounds dangerous, but I'm certain I can do it…."

*PEG,* eyes mischievous, scarlet lips pursed and inviting, pulled him to her again; she crossed her knees and the hem of her dress fell above their sleek curves, toward the tops of her sheer stockings.

Ross felt his heart jump as the sensuous parabola of her breast softened against his elbow, brushed his arm like a stolen kiss.

But while Peg kissed him, her sister strained away, white-lipped and silent, eyes turned to the wall.

They were jealous of each other; Ross had known that all along... since he'd first met them months ago; when their college professor in psychology had drawn his attention to the precise similarity with which their minds worked over any problem whatever.

Yes—he knew they were jealous. But he couldn't afford to antagonize either of them; he must be impartial. Even though he loved Mary with as much ardor as he'd ever felt for any woman, he mustn't let Peg know that until his plan was executed and he could choose in safety.

He withdrew from Peg's eager embrace and stepped back from the divan. "Well...?"

Mary's dark head bowed; her hands clenched at her breast. Her parted lips quivered and her breath caught sobbingly. But Peg smiled sardonically, looking up at him.

"Why not, darling?" she said easily. "I'm willing to let you operate."

And because Mary loved Ross more than her own life, she was willing, too.

Ross kissed them both; and even with his lips on Mary's, he met the knowing question in Peg's green eyes with a faint assenting nod.

*THE* round-the-world honeymoon cruise was almost over; and Nathan Ross was happy—or nearly so. He had fame; he had love and Mary; he had enough money. If it hadn't been for that letter that had so upset Mary....

Her sister had disappeared; weeks ago, though the letter from her mother had reached them only three days since in Havana.

Ross turned from the port of their luxurious stateroom on A-deck and dropped upon the satin coverlet of the bunk, beside Mary.

"I wouldn't worry, my sweet," Ross advised—easily enough, for he wasn't worrying. "What if she has cut loose from your mother? That doesn't mean anything has happened to her, you know. She's probably having a good time; taking advantage of her new freedom—just as you did."

Watching the way the semi-sheer pajama slicked its cerise, skin-like mould over the tapering round of her thigh, as she lay half on her side and half face down, Ross didn't care if Peg never did show up. Except for the way it was making Mary feel. He liked her to be cheerful, as she had been before this; gay, eager, ardent, with all her thoughts linked to his…. He let his knee touch hers.

Mary sat up and drew him to her. "Of course I'm not worrying," she said softly. "It's just that—oh, you will try to find her, won't you, sweetheart?"

"Yes," Ross assured her. "I'll try. So put it out of your mind."

He slid his hand from her waist, up the warm hollow of her back, and pulled her closer until he could feel the small delicious weight of one breast against him. Then she was fully in his arms, and his body was reacting to the softness of hers, thrilling to the glow of her skin beneath the web-fine mesh of her pajamas.

The long length of her legs slipped down as she kicked off her slippers and tucked her bare feet up on the bunk. She whispered

*He stared in horror. She was beginning to look almost like his wife!*

in his ear, sent a tense shiver down his spine by the caress of her breath against his cheek. And she sighed as he caught the ripe softness of her mouth with his hungry kiss.

Her bare arms tightened spasmodically about his neck and she quivered in his embrace when his lips sought the excited pulse fluttering in her throat.

No, Nathan Ross was not in a mood to worry, just now, about Mary's sister....

*BUT* four days later he changed his mind. Worrying was just what he was going to do from now on; he could see that.

For Peg Castle had been picked up by the police; turned over to the psychiatric ward. And the first person the police thought of, once they had learned her history, was the doctor who had performed the operation. It was from the date of that famous event, as nearly as they could tell, that Peg had gone to hell—or almost there. The vice squad had hauled her in.

And Ross examined her the same morning Mary had recounted her terrible dream. "Hold me tight, don't let me go back to sleep!" she had whimpered. "I dreamed some other girl had taken you away from me. I—I dreamed that other men—more than one—were making love to me. And I liked the idea because I wanted to get revenge on you."

Odd dream. Ross had started a tentative analysis, frowned at possibilities he didn't enjoy admitting, and ceased questioning her.

And now here was Peg, with the police blotter recording experiences that sounded almost like Mary's dream!

But Peg was defiantly gay—though her lips were compressed; contorted down at the corners in a derisive grimace.

"Well, sweetheart—they've hooked me haven't they?"

They were in his uptown office. Her dress was cheap and cut to show too much of her ripely curved, slender figure. As she edged closer to him, her hips rippled and swayed in a careless wanton swing; and her plump, firm breasts, covered only by the blouse, defied his eyes to stay away.

They didn't. Ross felt the heat of his humming blood inflame his brain. Could this be Peg?—the sister of his demure, naive wife! This gamin, this girl of the streets who invited him with her eyes, her posture, the faint nudge of her knee against his as she leaned against him.

"Peg!" He took her shoulders sternly, shook her. "What's the matter with you? What's happened to you?"

Her manner changed abruptly; her voice became terribly normal—almost like her old voice. "You know damned well what it is, you rat!" she almost whispered. "You know what you did to me…! You let me think you'd marry me… until it was too late; then you married Mary. Yes, you low louse—I'm still crazy about you. I always was; and if I can't have you, there are other men! That's what's wrong with me!"

**SUDDENLY** she clutched at him, her nails biting into the back of his neck, while her mouth parted and forced its moist writhing warmth into his lips. Her whole body moulded to his, clinging with every lovely contour until his arms involuntarily crushed her close. "Now what?" she murmured, her breath mingling with his.

He thrust her away violently. "Now what?" he mocked violently. "Now you're off your head, and I'm going to cure you—before the police lock you up for good."

"Yeah? What are you going to do?"

"I'll talk to you." Ross was in a cold sweat. "I'll hypnotize you."

"Like hell!" Peg said calmly. She lit a cigarette. "You double-crossing punk! So it was my sister you loved after all. To hell with you!"

He had to do something about her, Ross knew. He couldn't have disintegration of morals, slackening of the intelligence;—or whatever this all was—entered as a result in the follow-ups of his operation. And he'd have a wild woman for a wife if Mary knew all about Peg.

Ross changed tactics. "Forgive me, Peg." His mouth twisted bitterly, the jaw muscles twitched. "There's no use denying it—I did make a hell of a mistake, and I feel it now—plenty!" Win her confidence—that was it; he had to get her on his side somehow, and this was the best way.

"Why did you think I sent you away? It was because I was afraid of you! Why do you think I'm so bitter about all this—the police reports, the things you've been doing... the other men! Jealous! I might as well admit it; I've been thinking of you constantly—almost since the very day I sailed away with Mary."

"Have you, Nat?" Her voice was eager, her eyes hungry, and she was in his arms again.

Assurance with kisses—that's what she had to have, Ross told himself. And he wanted to assure her. And the longer he held her in his arms, the better he felt about it.

There was something abandoned, unreserved about Peg's frank ardor that Mary didn't have. And of course this was the only way he could get her to submit to his treatment; he had to do his best, for her sake, for his own sake, for Mary's too. And for the police.

Ross scooped her up in his arms with his wrist caught in the wedge of her knees, behind them, locked warmly by her thighs and calves.

He held her high, luxuriating in the sensuous pressure of her body against his chest. He sat down suddenly in a deep arm chair, with the weight of her body delightfully oppressing his in every point of contact.

She wasn't waiting for him; she was kissing him madly, almost eating his lips with hers, hugging herself to him until the two of them were almost like one.

Ross was thinking of Mary—and all the people for whose benefit he had to permit himself the indulgence of Peg's frenzied love-making, and presently he was thinking only of Peg—and himself. Most of all, of himself....

**"YOU'RE** drowsy..." intoned Ross, leaning over the recumbent form of Peg. "You're getting drowsy... drowsier... sleepier and sleepier. When I have counted ten, you will be deeply asleep... asleep...."

She trusted him now; it was easy to hypnotize her, even to the deepest stage of somnambulism.

And he encouraged her to talk in her hypnotic sleep; to unburden her heart. "Ah, darling, I'm so glad we're married… so glad!"

Well, that was all right, Ross assured himself; a simple wishfulfilment impulse to dream she was married to him. Only he couldn't let her persist in it. She breathed quietly for a minute without speaking, and he didn't prompt her. But suddenly a cold wet breeze seemed to bathe him in clammy sweat. Her face! Why, she was beginning to look almost—almost like Mary—as Mary had this morning when he had left her!

Ross stared, breathing hoarsely. They were twins, it was true, but they didn't look identical. Yet now, within the space of a couple of minutes—since she had begun thinking of herself as married to him—Peg was looking like Mary!

"… So glad we're married at last," the entranced girl murmured again. "For darling, I have to confess it now—I was so afraid you'd marry Peg instead! Something—maybe the way you used to kiss her sometimes differently from the way you kissed me—told me you loved her more. But you don't, do you?"

Ross drew in a long, fluttering breath and clutched his trembling hands together. Those were the *very words* that Mary had spoken to him the first day of their honeymoon! And there couldn't have been any way for Peg to have heard them. Why, Mary didn't even know her sister had been found, yet.

Peg's face colored with a blush; she looked in that moment almost like Mary herself! She shivered a little and murmured:

"Ah, my sweet, I like the way you kiss me there… between the shoulders!" She bit her lips and trembled, and she murmured and whispered more words—words that no lips but Mary's had uttered before, and no ears but Ross's had heard.

*IN* five minutes, Ross found himself gripping the seat of his chair, nails clawing the upholstery. His jaws were painfully tense, his teeth grinding. "Wake up!" he cried. "Wake up!" He heard a gasp. Then, "So, darling—have you cured me already?" in the hard, derisive tones of Peg.

He stared at her—stared at the girl who now looked like

herself; bitter and hard—but not so much as before he had kissed her today. She came into his arms gently, and feeling her pouting lips clasp and part against his mouth, he hardly knew which girl he was kissing....

He tasted blood, inside his lips. He jerked back.

"What's that—what cut your mouth?"

Peg drew a hand mirror from her bag. Then she said, half joking, but strangely frightened, "What did? It must have been your rough kiss, wasn't it?"

But the cut, the abrasion, extended from the soft skin of her mouth, diagonally across her upper lip to her cheek. No kiss could have caused it.

*ROSS* decided not to tell Mary about Peg quite yet. Chances were, she'd learn about it from the police, the newspapers, or the like. But until then—

When he entered their apartment and bent to kiss her that evening, Ross jumped back and a cry leaped from his lips.

"Great God, Mary—*where did you get that cut?*"

Mary frowned—and when she frowned, her usually tender mouth looked almost as bitter, as derisively twisted, as Peg's. She put her fingers to her face.

The cut extended diagonally across her upper lip to her cheek.

"It's nothing"—her laugh seemed one of annoyance—"nothing but a scratch. I stumbled and hit the corner of a table. That sounds funny, but you act as if I'd broken my neck."

Ross almost wished she had.

*BY* the end of the third week, Ross wasn't sure whether he was still sane.

Through some miracle of chance, Mary didn't yet know that her sister had been found. Yet, equally strange, she ceased to worry about her.

Peg had responded *too* well to hypnotic treatment. At Ross's suggestions, she gradually forgot details of the life she had led during the past year. But at the same time she began to remember more and more of what rightfully should have been only inside Mary's mind.

Once she said: "Don't forget the theater tonight." And that evening, Mary greeted him with: "I forgot to tell you, sweetheart, that I'd bought theater tickets for tonight.... Why what's wrong about that? You look like a ghost!"

And as Peg acquired the knowledge that belonged only in Mary's mind, she came to look more and more nearly like her. At the same time, Mary came to possess oftener that hard, bitter look that really belonged to Peg; her dreams were of evil things—were, in fact, composed of all details that Ross had been hypnotizing Peg into forgetting!

The psychiatrist for the city was pleased with the change Ross had wrought in Peg.

"Another week," Ross advised. "It needs that long at least."

And the next day, leaning over Peg, he suggested, over and over:

"You're remembering now; it's all coming back to you... those weeks you spent with Kurt, and with Lily Martin; you did do those things; you remember now, don't you?"

And Peg remembered. She began to look like herself. Began to think differently, remember differently....

For—though he hated to think of believing such stuff—Ross thought it was plain enough: Somehow the personalities of the twin sisters had been interflowing, to some degree, until he separated them. When they had divided, the evil had predominated in Peg, the good in Mary. Though of course you couldn't call everything good or evil as casually as that. Still, that was the way it had turned out.

*WITHIN* a week, Peg was Peg again—and Mary was Mary, without those fearful dreams and evil tendencies that struck her and transformed her into another woman.

And then—

"Damn you to hell— I know what's been happening! I know what you've done!" flared Peg. "You were getting to love me—and

*"I'll have Jake's gang kill you!"*
*she snarled as he seized her*
*and threw her from him.*

now you've made me different, and you've gone back to *her!* I'll kill you! I'll have Jake's gang beat you to a pulp! I'll—"

She sprang at him clawing, ripping at his face with angry nails; high heels stamping around his toes. Ross grabbed her, picked her up squirming and screaming, and threw her down upon the couch with enough force to knock her breathless.

He leaned close to her, looked into her eyes.

"Go to sleep!" he said sharply. And instantly Peg relaxed and sank into her somnambulistic trance. Then Ross began to murder her with subtle swiftness.

He didn't kill her with a bullet or a knife, and he didn't strangle her. He knew a better way. He instilled in her mind a simple suggestion; a hypnotically induced obsession.

"On your way back to the hospital tonight, you will freeze

motionless whenever you hear an automobile horn or trolley car beside you; you will be unable to move until someone touches you."

Two or three times he repeated it, in different phrasing, questioning her until he was assured she understood.

For now Ross was afraid of her. He would destroy her, wipe out the evil part of the Castle twins' character… destroy this occult connection—be it telepathic, clairvoyant, or what—and have Mary again for himself as she should be!

*THE* instant Ross saw his wife, he knew he had been successful in his murder. For all the evil hardness and bitterness that had ever shone in Peg's face now stamped Mary's. He had got Peg killed by an auto or a street car; but only the body had died; that spirit which belonged to both girls now resided entirely in Mary. And all the thwarted love Peg had had for him still lived.

Mary threw herself in his arms, with embraces and gestures that belonged only to Peg; kissed him in open-mouthed abandon, with tricks of her lips that only Peg had known, her hips trembled against him; her breasts flattened upon his chest, and she moaned into his mouth.

In the first burst of horror and anger, Ross flung her half across the room. For a few seconds he almost believed that this was the same girl he had left half an hour before, the girl he had sent to her death. Then he saw that, though she acted like Peg and looked nearly like her—she was still Mary.

"My darling!" he groaned, stumbling forward, clasping his arms about her knees abjectly. "Forgive me."

"You can go to hell!" The girl's voice was raspy and hard.

She disappeared into her boudoir, reappeared with her coat and flounced out of the room without looking at him. After long, dull minutes, Ross followed her. She wasn't in sight on the street below, but instinctively he knew where he would find her.

*IT* took him fifteen minutes by cab to reach the neighborhood he sought. He walked three blocks and came to the house whose number he had dragged up from the recesses of his mind and Peg's police record.

The girl who opened the door was too old to be as young as she obviously was. Her lips and hair were red. Her skin looked pale green in the dim light.

"You Lily Martin?" Ross smiled.

"Who wants to know?" Her eyes narrowed to gleams of suspicion.

Ross shrugged. "Friend of mine told me to ask for you. Said we ought to get on well together."

"What friend?"

"Her name is—Peg. 'Least I call her that."

"Yeah?" The girl smiled, finally. "Well, come on in."

The girl took him to a room leading off the back of the hallway. "So Peg sent you here, eh? Well, do you like me?"

The wrapper dropped from her and she stood very close to him, her heavy yet well-contoured breasts rising and falling with her breathing, almost touching him. Pink lace step-ins hugged her full hips, and dark stockings clung tautly to the long sweep of her legs, snugly secured by laced garters high on her smooth thighs.

"Sure I like you!" Ross pulled her against him, held her tight and kissed her. He was breathing harshly; but he was listening to faint voices that seemed to come from the adjoining room.

Presently, Lily Martin whispered: "What's Peg to you, honey?"

Ross's nerves screamed. He flung her away from him and cried wildly: "She's—*my wife!*"

And he pulled open the door, ran into the hall, and crashed himself against the next door. Her voice again… the hard, derisive, laughing voice of Peg—no, of Mary—of both!

The door didn't break, but it was jerked open and Ross staggered into the room.

*HIS* wife was directly across the room from him—not cowering, but brazenly flaunting herself before him and the man who had opened the door. Only tailored step-ins encased her hips, and her stockings were torn down. The rouge from her lips was smeared in spots over her face. She didn't look much like Mary now—almost all like Peg.

Ross, hair disheveled, eyes glazing, started toward her with a groan of despair. She spat at him and yelled harshly:

"This is him, Jake! This is the rat I told you about! Git 'im!"

Then there was more than one man, more than the thick-chested, grizzle-jawed mug who had opened the door. They fell on Ross from behind, from the front. They beat him to a pulp.

The last thing he heard on this earth was Peg's raucous laugh ringing in his ears… ringing… ringing….

E. HOFFMANN PRICE

# hands of the dead

*He was an unscrupulous, blood-thirsty*
*bandit. Only one goal existed for him—to*
*avenge his dead brother. And even the poor*
*missionary's daughter fell under the spell*
*of his vehemence, and his taking ways*

*H*OOFS THUNDERED, and spurts of yellow
flame were followed by a ragged crackle of rifle fire which
accented the savage yelling that came out of the night and closed
in on the Gibson Memorial Mission. Hell was roaring, north of
the Hei Lung Chiang—the Black Dragon River that winds its
crooked course across northern Manchuria.

Velma Gibson, daughter of the founder of the medical mission,
was on her feet at the first alarm. Her thin nightgown could not
quite mask the supple curve of her waist or the quiver of her pert
breasts; and before it settled to her ankles, its sudden disarray
displayed legs that would have become a tradition on Broadway.

She was worried, but confident. Carrying on since her father's
death, dispensing pills and civilization, she had more than once
dissuaded bandits from looting the mission.

Her sweet, serious face was framed with black hair that trailed
down to rounded hips which deserved clinging silks, not the
practical garments she hastily donned after her discarded gown
had left her slim young form clothed for a moment only in her
shimmering web of smoky dark hair.

Below, the compound was in an uproar. As she raced downstairs, bullets showered her with splinters of wood. And above
the confusion, she caught the name of Hong Wu, the bandit who
had become a war lord.

Her servants, howling and chattering, fled to the rear. Velma
hurried toward the compound gate. The mission was unarmed.
In less troubled times, her father's benevolence and trusting at-

titude had been justified. She believed in it herself, but that belief was wavering.

"I am Hong Wu!" a voice boomed above the yelling and tramping outside. "Open up—or would you rather be roasted out?"

Peering through the cracks in the heavy gate, she saw the bandit chief in the full glare of newly lighted torches. He was squat and stocky, and his pudgy face was as cruel as his piggish eyes.

"Just a minute!" she temporized, making a show of fumbling with the heavy bars. "We have food, but no money. Take what you want, but don't let your men ruin the medical stores. If you have any wounded, we'll treat them."

That might work. If not, nothing else could. Hong Wu laughed, then singsonged an order in Chinese. The yells of his men subsided. Heart hammering, Velma tugged at the bar. But before it yielded, her blood froze.

*FROM* the second story of the mission came a dull boom. Slugs whistled over the compound. A bandit dropped his torch. Another cursed, his face a red blot as he reeled in the saddle. One of her servants, running amuck, had found her father's old shotgun.

Another blast. And then, from outside, came a shrill screaming, the crackling of rifles, the crunch of gun butts. Recoiling in terror, Velma saw one of her servants about to clear the crest of the wall, lurch back, riddled and kicking. In desperation, one of them had fired in order to create a distraction while the others fled, hoping to escape cross country. But the cries that followed were an agonizing testimonial to that futile stratagem.

Rifles were crackling. Gun butts hammered against the gate. Torches were hurled over the compound wall. Since the sharpened stakes made scaling difficult, fire would force the occupants out.

Velma dashed into the house and up toward her *amah's* room. In the confusion of looting she might slip out.

The gate was creaking under heavy blows. They had improvised a battering ram. Disguised, she would have a better chance. She discarded her dress, and for a moment she stood in that chilly room, tightly binding her breasts, subduing their soft young curves to mimic the flat-chestedness affected by Chinese women. A jacket—another—and a third—

The door burst open before her costuming was complete. Velma cried out, turned toward the window; but it was only the *amah*, frantically jabbering: "Help is on the way—I saw them—listen—"

The distant drumming of hoofs blended with the whiplash smack of carbines, the thunder of pistols. The exultant howls of Hong Wu's men changed to frantic yells, as they discarded their torches. Leaning recklessly from the window, Velma saw a dark mass of men and horses, gleaming blades, rifles gushing flame.

Men were dropping as they tried to mount and ride. Hong Wu's raiders were in full rout.

"Thank God!" she devoutly exclaimed.

But the little *amah* was not so optimistic: "Maybe someone worse. Or Hong Wu would not be afraid."

*While he drank, she prayed to a god unknown by her father—the god of wrath!*

*A TALL* man in a shaggy sheepskin coat towered above the hard riding pursuers who pulled up beside the mission. By the flame of a blazing storehouse, Velma saw his grim, craggy face. He was an American, but he shouted orders in Chinese as fluent as her own.

Then he caught a glimpse of Velma, and penetrated her incomplete disguise. He hailed her in English, "Hi, there! Miss Gibson, aren't you? I had a hunch Hong Wu was going to loot the mission. Hang on—be back later—I'll leave Wang Lee and a few men to put out the fire—got to nail Hong Wu—"

His horse bounded forward as he spoke the last words. The iron promise in his voice made her shiver, even though he had saved the mission.

A squad in command of a lean, handsome Manchu remained behind. They methodically made their, way from one fallen bandit to the next. A pistol shot or a sword stroke; calm, systematic butchery, mechanical in its rhythm.

This American soldier of fortune might be worse than Hong Wu. China was full of renegade Americans who were more barbarous than the natives. But the *amah* was beaming: "Ah, there is a man!"

Velma shuddered, and reproved, "That's awful! Get some bandages—maybe we can save a few—"

Her father's benevolent spirit, however, did not have a chance. Before Velma reached the compound gate, she would have needed baskets, not bandages for her fallen enemies.

But her wounded servants took the next few hours of her time.

She returned to her own room, and horror was faintly diluted by recollection of the momentary flash of friendliness that had brightened the American's grim face. Maybe he could be persuaded from his savagery.

Velma wriggled out of her Chinese costume, loosened the bindings that marred the rounded loveliness of her breasts and slipped into a robe. Not even a life wholly devoted to service had blinded her to the fact that she had exquisite legs. She dug up a pair of long unused silk hosiery, and as she drew them on, she logically enough reasoned that her sleek curves might help the savage American see the sublime truths in her arguments on mercy to wounded enemies. At all events, she wanted to be presentable when she thanked him.

She exhumed a little bottle of perfume hoarded from some almost forgotten Christmas, and touched its stopper behind her ears and for good measure, put a dab between the delicious curves that a brassiere did not quite subdue.

Though she had only three dresses, the selection required thought.

*VELMA,* duplicated in the mirror that reflected every lithe curve from her ankles to her throat, began to sense that she would be uncommonly persuasive. But it was late, and maybe the rescue party would not return that night. Then, as she debated this matter of waiting, the door swung softly open.

She cried out, made a dive for her discarded robe. The intruder was Wang Lee, the American's Chinese lieutenant. "General Bennett," he announced, "will be away some time, pursuing the enemy who killed his brother."

Wang Lee's eyes told her that the lieutenant had no intention of wasting valuable opportunity.

"Please go out until I'm dressed. Can't you see—"

"Plenty, but not enough," he countered. "What I saw from the roof of the storehouse while putting out the blaze has started another fire."

Velma reddened at least to her hips. What Wang hadn't seen—! Before she could decide which way to turn, he had an armful and wouldn't let go.

She kicked his shins wildly, crisscrossed his face with her nails until he looked like a tomcat returning from a tough weekend; but Wang Lee was squeezing her breathless, at the same time tearing at the film of chiffon that was to have been the foundation of a lecture on civilization. Once she broke away, and smacked down on his head with a wash basin.

He sank to his knees, and as he recovered, she cried out, "You fool—when the general returns—"

"He won't be back for a long time!" gasped Wang. Then it occurred to him that his chief would eventually hear plenty. He had gone entirely too far. Fear and wrath were now blended with his pleasanter emotions. "He'll never know!"

Her next blow was glancing. Wang ducked, tackling her about the knees. They crashed into a corner. The room was whirling; Velma's breath came in sobbing gasps. Before this was over, she'd be glad to die!

Neither she nor her assailant heard the tramp of booted feet in the hall. A stern voice grated, "I told you that that stuff is out. And I meant it!"

**GENERAL BENNETT** had returned. His eyes were black as the muzzle of the pistol in his hand. He jerked Wang to his feet; and before Velma's assailant could recover from the shock of the unexpected meeting, there was a muffled explosion. The top of Wang's head was blasted off, spattered horribly over the wallpaper.

"Sorry he bothered you," smiled Bennett, gesturing for his men to withdraw.

*The shadows were not too clear, yet they set Velma's heart afire.*

Velma stared. He was deadly as a tiger, and as handsome. She wondered at the silver case that peeped from the collar of his shaggy sheepskin coat. It was the size and shape of a man's hand, and hung from his neck like a reliquary.

"I'm ever so grateful." She shivered, yet could not force herself to brush away the blood and brain spatters that flecked breasts and shoulders, leaving traces of red against creamy white. "But—your methods—are—"

He understood, and cut into her fumbling for speech. "I've heard of you. And your father. But listen, darling—turning the other cheek doesn't work in China." As he resumed, he fingered the strange silver hand at his chest. "Hong Wu captured my brother for ransom. I couldn't raise the money. So he sent me a hand as a reminder. I preserved it in this case. Later, we found the body. They'd killed him because of too hot pursuit."

"Ohhh—" She shuddered. "Terrible. But—you're a white man."

"Forget it! I have. That's why I'm leading the advance guard of the Northern Route Army. To capture Hong Wu."

"But your men butchered those wounded bandits," she began. "Most of them are just farmers, made desperate by poverty."

"I told them to. I've sworn to carve the gizzard out of Hong Wu and every man that follows him. That's why they checked out when they heard I was on the trail."

Bennett regarded her with amused tolerance. Her long hair covered more than her remaining few shreds of clothing; but she felt that she was safe from that vengeance crazed man. His wrath kept his mind from women.

"And if I do stop a bullet before I lay my hands on Hong Wu," he continued, handing her the discarded robe, "by God, I'll come out of my grave to finish him!"

He spoke with a terrible solemnity. For a moment she believed that he could do that very thing. His blazing eyes had the fascination of a tiger's. And though she absent-mindedly fumbled with the edges of her robe, hiding her bruised legs and clawed body, she could not draw away from his gaze.

A deep seated, primitive glow flamed up and blotted out her horror of his methodical slayings. His presence was gripping her, before she realized it, she was wondering how it would feel to be caressed by those deadly hands.

He abruptly resumed, "Better hurry and pack up."

"Why?"

"Because I'm burning the mission."

*"What?"* She recoiled.

"Hong Wu is hard pressed. You have stores, medicine, food. I can't risk his sending some raiders back to get any such advantage. Neither can I leave a guard here to protect you."

"But you can't!" she protested. "The people around here—they're harmless—they need us—they—"

"Tough luck, sister." He was almost sympathetic. "But I told you, I'm getting Hong Wu if I have to reach from my grave to throttle him."

"You're blasphemous—beastly—savage!" she flared, eyes blazing.

He tapped the gruesome silver memento on his chest, and countered, "All right, I am. And you're a plain damn' fool. Sticking around here, you'd end up with some of what Wang Lee was trying to dish out."

"But what'll I do if you burn—"

"Follow the Northern Route Army. There's going to be hell roaring from now on. You haven't a chance."

Thus, an hour later, all that remained of the Gibson Memorial Mission was Velma and her ideals. Her amah, huddled into a creaking escort wagon, kept her company.

*DURING* the next week's march into northern Manchuria, she saw little of Bennett. There were skirmishes, attacks and counter attacks; and from her cramped quarters in the wagon, Velma saw things for which not even her years in China had prepared her.

Files of captives, wrists lashed, knelt in long rows as the executioner trotted down the line, a sword stroke slicing off a head at every other pace. Once, Bennett himself, after staring at one of the averted faces, snatched the blade and deftly took a swing. Then he returned it; he was interested only in Hong Wu's relatives.

*He clawed and bit and struck, but she was his match.*

And once, as the wagon rolled past his pavilion, she caught a glimpse of a slender girl, her graceful figure silhouetted against the tent wall. Bennett's evenings apparently were too busy to leave him any thoughts for Velma. She shivered... a white man, beheading captives, fondling Chinese girls, smoking opium... then she laughed metallically. This was the man she had thought of reforming; this was the one whose dynamic presence had stirred her to the depths of her being, for a moment, a moment which he could have lengthened, if his hands had not been red with murder, and his eyes agleam with vengeance.

One night, when the wind mercilessly searched every leak in the wagon tarpaulin, Velma persuaded a teamster to move it to the sheltered side of a knoll. But even there she lay shivering in the chill. The memory of Bennett's quizzical glance that had appraised every line and curve of her as he booted his dead lieutenant aside made her blood race. It was becoming increasingly difficult to fight off Bennett's personality. Slaughter, through sheer repetition, was lulling her indignation.

And then furtive voices filtered into the wagon as the wind for a moment ceased howling.

"Ch'ing Hsing will attend to that foreign devil who butchered my uncle, Wang Lee…."

"But how, Honorable Lu?"

Vengeance and treachery were seeking Bennett. The conspirators, finding shelter under what they thought, was a ration wagon, were directly beneath Velma.

Ch'ing Hsing—Bright Star, the name meant. Whoever that was, she had to warn him. Saving her from the lieutenant had caused this conspiracy. She could not let him fall into a trap.

Yet once she spoke, the camp would run red with blood. She remembered the heads Bennett had placed on poles thrust into the river mud; faces grinning, mouths wide open, teeth agleam in the moonlight; and shocks of black hair, matted with gore….

One word from her, and it would be as though she herself had swung the sword. Human life, somehow, was still sacred to Velma. She could not warn Bennett without giving him details; otherwise he would laugh, gay and grim.

The wind blotted out the rest of the plot. She dared not stir, lest they realize she had heard, and kill her. But finally, she distinguished two dark figures scurrying around the knoll.

Heart hammering, she emerged from her heap of sheepskin rugs, slipped into a coat, and crept out into the darkness. Unperceived, she passed groups squatting about dying fires. If it were learned that she had had a hand in exposing the plot, vengeance would find her, no matter what efforts Bennett made toward protecting her.

*SENTRIES* with fixed bayonets were on guard about his tent. She flattened into the shadow of a heap of boxed three inch shells, and waited, counting the measured paces, back and forth. A small, sharp knife gleamed in her hand.

One bound across the two yard space, and she would slit the tent, creeping, warn him, then leave. But even as her muscles tensed, she checked herself, listening.

Bennett was not alone. She heard a woman's laughter, then a stirring, and an inner light cast shadows on the tent wall as the occupants shifted. The woman was slender, and wore an ornate headdress which she was trying to protect from Bennett's hearty caresses. Bennett must be very much in love with her....

The shadows were not too explicit, yet they set Velma afire to her very marrow, and her breath was quickening. Once, it seemed that that girl was reaching for a hairpin that would stab a man to the heart. But before Velma could recklessly dash from cover, she saw an empty hand stroking his cheek.

Then, as the wind left a little gap in its howling, she heard Bennett say, "Don't be silly, Ch'ing Hsing—I haven't the least time for that white girl—she's too inhumanly pious and her blood is ice water—"

Ch'ing Hsing, the Bright Star, was the assassin sent to kill Bennett.

Velma's lovely face was tense, her eyes were bright, and her breasts rose and fell with more than natural breathing as she emerged from cover and deliberately walked toward the front of the tent. There, as the sentry snapped his rifle to the ready, she lowered the scarf that muffled her face and said, "Tell the general I wish to see him at once."

Her plans had changed. She could block the Bright Star without having the executioner work overtime.. And she told herself that what she planned was mainly to save a number of lives....

Bennett, quizzical and a little annoyed, emerged from the rear of the tent, stood in the front section and curiously regarded her.

"Dave—" Then she desperately blurted it out: "Dave—I've been terribly mean to you—if you'd promise me—you'd leave those native women alone—I'd—"

Her cheeks were aflame, and she knew that she must be red down to her ankles. He brightened, and said, "I was hoping you'd not keep on despising me—"

"I don't—I really never did—" She was in his arms, clinging close.

"Gorgeous!" he breathed, stroking her black ringlets and looking down at her upturned face for a moment. Then he felt the violent tremor of her body, and caught the desperate light in her eyes. He frowned, shook his head. "Your heart isn't in this. Why—"

"Don't ask me!" She tiptoed, and her kiss blotted out his query. He must not suspect. If he did, he'd force the truth from her, and

*She fought him savagely with every weapon at her disposal.*

she would be responsible for deadly wrath that would follow. "I—I just want to, that's all—"

Her warmth and fragrance dizzied him, and every supple curve that clung to him cried silently for his caresses. Bennett, the tiger of Manchuria, was no match for this lovely fanatic whose purpose wore the guise of love. She was shameless in her artifices, playing her part so well that she was no longer acting. He couldn't doubt the ripple of her perfect body, the renting gasps that forced her breast against him, reminding him that she was nicer than that straight-lined Chinese sing-song girl…. Bennett's blood was racing from that embrace, and its reminders of things he had almost forgotten: the white loveliness and clean scent of a woman of his own race, untainted by Asiatic perfumes and cosmetics.

*BUT* Ch'ing Hsing was in the rear section of his pavilion. He did not suspect that Velma knew of her presence. To know of his native playmates was one thing; but to see one leaving, right before her eyes—that would be too much!

"Wait—just a second, darling!" He disengaged her arms, clapped his hands. "I've got to sign a few field orders." Then, as an orderly entered in response to his summons, he said, "Tsin Hai, stand by for dispatches."

Ch'ing Hsing did not speak English. She might not have understood. As they stepped toward the rear, Bennett whispered a few words to the orderly: "Take that sing-song girl out the back. Knock her cold if she lets out a yeep!"

His strategy, however, was wasted. The yellow-skinned beauty was not in the rear section of the large tent. She must have realized from Bennett's voice that she was no longer wanted; and since the heart of a sing-song girl is rarely involved, she had tactfully faded.

The only sign of her presence was a bottle of Scotch and two glasses, one stained with lip rouge. Bennett drank both, then tossed the red-edged one out beneath the tent wall. That one trace of Ch'ing Hsing removed, he handed the orderly a sheaf of dummy papers, and followed him to the front. There Bennett found Velma near the flap, twisting a handkerchief. He did not suspect that she had done her best to make it easy for him to get rid of the sing-song girl.

They were both happy; particularly Velma, whose conscience now would not be branded with murder. But, as Bennett's arms closed about her, vivid sensations that raced through her blood made her anything but a sacrifice to prevent slaughter.

Whatever qualms she may have had were melting in that warm gloom, where Bennett, awkward and almost shy, knelt beside that palpitant white length of loveliness...."

"Maybe," he muttered, a long time after, "I might lay off wholesale beheadings. But I can't quit hunting Hong Wu. My brother was alive when his hand was chopped off."

"But, darling—" And now she was not shamming. "Could you forgive—"

"No, damn it!" he growled. "Have you ever had someone you loved savagely murdered? If your father had been butchered instead of dying in bed—"

"Let's talk about something else," she whispered, arms and lips seeking him.

"Drink?" he wondered, finding a second glass and filling both.

"You might know I never touch liquor," she smiled. "Take a kiss instead...."

It seemed almost wicked, finding sacrifice so glorious....

But that ended before sunrise. Death stalked into Bennett's tent; not the assassin's knife or bullet, but poison that gripped the soldier of fortune with corrosive fangs.

*HOURS* later, Velma heard the surgeon's verdict: no antidote would work, and death agonizing hours distant. Bennett's face, now gray-green and clammy, had frozen into a mask that she could not endure seeing.

At last he was able to say to a trusted *aide*, "Keep this secret. If the news gets out, my men will scatter, and Hong Wu will escape. Shoot me if I make any betraying sound. Get ready to attack. Maybe—you can—bring me—his head—before I die."

An hour passed. The *aide* returned to the tent. Two officers accompanied him, dragging a gory, broken bundle they tossed to the floor. It quivered and wheezed. It could no longer cry out.

Velma, sick with horror, saw that it was what remained of a woman: Ch'ing Hsing. The *aide* confirmed her guess, and said to Bennett, "August and Heaven-Sent General, I overheard an orderly wondering about this woman's sudden disappearance from your tent. I also wondered, and thus a picket halted her. When your illness began, we questioned her, and after the first hundred cuts, she spoke. Thorns driven under her nails helped somewhat.

"The cousin of Wang Lee—that insignificant person whose head you were pleased to blow skyward at the mission—conspired with Hong Wu, and this sing-song girl was sent to poison your whiskey, which she did before leaving."

Velma's benevolent intentions and her father's precepts had betrayed her, had forged a deadly chain whose last link was the awful and lingering doom of the man she loved.

She was thinking alien thoughts as she heard the aide saying: "Exalted and Heaven-Born Superior, since your enemy knows that your death has been accomplished, it is best that we retreat before he attacks. Our men are already muttering their fears."

Bennett groaned through clenched teeth. His eyes were like live coals in a horrible grayish mask; but Velma looked him in the face and said: "Hong Wu can't *know* whether the plan succeeded. Not yet. And before he is sure, I will go into his camp and kill him."

"How?" Bennett just managed to articulate.

"Give me that silver hand. And some Chinese clothes. It is easy."

Later, when they were alone, he watched her arrange her long, black hair and paint her face and lips, chalk white and blazing scarlet. She washed bits of flesh from Ch'ing Hsing's jewelry and put it on.

"It's crazy—you don't look like her—" He clawed for words.

"I don't have to!" she flared. "I came to convert you, but it's worked the other way about. I'll kill Hong Wu. Even if you could reach from your grave. His raid on the mission is the root of all this."

Before dawn broke, she crept out into the darkness, leaving a warped, corroded lover to face death alone.

*HONG WU* lay stretched on a *k'ang* in the reception room of a *yamen* that had until recently belonged to a Manchu prince. Now the compound and all the rooms of the old palace were occupied by his bandit-soldiers, shock-headed ruffians who had befouled everything that they could not burn, or carry away to sell.

The outraged garden was dotted with fires around which they were cooking their supper. The air was heavy with the reek of opium that bubbled in the pipes of those who had already eaten; and Hong Wu was in the midst of his second pipe when a girl wearing a long, quilted coat passed the sentries who guarded his private apartment.

Velma Gibson had reached her destination. Her only weapon was one which a possible search would not betray; a slender blade, whose carved jade hilt projected from her hair as though it were part of her ornate headdress.

He looked up, regarding her with eyes contracted by opium. He laughed drunkenly, having reached the early stages of intoxication.

"Honorable Hong," she began, "I have news of General Bennett, who has sworn to take your head."

The bandit stroked his straggling mustache, set aside his pipe. "Was he killed in a skirmish?"

"No. He is well and unwounded. But if you will pay my father ten thousand *taels* in advance, I will catch Bennett off guard in his tent and kill him, And be glad to die for that stroke."

Hong Wu demanded, "How will you succeed where others have failed?"

"He trusts me," asserted Velma. Then, producing the silver reliquary, "And this proves it."

Hong Wu's eyes narrowed. He had often heard of the gruesome gage of vengeance, and said, "Let me have it. This is Bennett's luck. It is *feng shui*—the devil charm that protects him."

"No," protested Velma. "I stole it from him, to prove to you that I can approach him. But if I return without it, he'll kill me. Don't you see," she went on, playing up to the superstitious fear which Bennett had inspired, "if I am in his tent, I can strike before he gets the *feng shui* hand from me."

"Ten thousand *taels*?" Hong's hand reached out. "But I must see if this really contains a hand, before I send the money to your father."

This was her chance: strike when his glance shifted to the trophy. But as she drew the deceptive knife from her hair, there was a savage yell, a grunt and a gasp, and strong fingers closed about her wrist.

"Beware, Your Excellency!" panted the newcomer, struggling with Velma. "This is a trick—Bennett is dying—look!"

Thrusting the slim blade into his belt, he tore aside the trailing end of the head kerchief that half concealed Velma's face. Attracted by the scuffle, two sentries came running in. Her assailant, mud-splashed and wounded, addressed Hong Wu: "The sing-song girl was tortured until she betrayed the cousin of Wang Lee. This woman came to kill you. I heard, while hiding and waiting for my chance to escape and slip through the lines. Look again, Exalted Commander!"

*HONG WU* watched the sentries tearing the first three jackets from Velma. They had her peeled down to her sheer, white undergarment; and it was torn to shreds by their clawing hands. They stripped off her breast bindings, exposing full, white curves which proved that she was not Chinese; and in the struggle, the make-up that had disguised her face and eyes was ruined, completing her betrayal.

Bitterness blotted out the terror in her heart. One conspirator, unaccounted for in the confusion following Bennett's agony, had upset her plan. She had assumed that her lover's *aide* had uncovered the whole plot, had dealt with all three as he had with the sing-song girl. Hong Wu read her thought, and chuckled venomously.

"No weapons hidden in the odds and ends you've not torn from her. Now get out, sons of turtles! Close the door and don't come back till I send for you. I am going to question her about Bennett's plans."

The sentries and the fugitive withdrew, leaving Velma with Hong Wu, whose evening opium had inflamed his blood to fever pitch. There was much to be done before she was flayed alive, or pierced with sharp slivers of bamboo.

"It will bring me more luck, this capturing Bennett's woman," laughed Hong Wu, watching the flame of the opium lamp cast wavering lights on her shapely legs and white body as she recovered enough from the mauling to try to regain her feet.

Velma wavered dizzily, flashed a despairing glance about her. She saw a door that opened from the rear of the room. Better be killed by some startled sentry as she fled.

She was scarcely half way to her slender chance when Hong Wu overtook her. Velma's shuddering scream drowned his lustful mutterings. Desperately she clawed and scratched, kicked and bit, but opium inspiration and the resilient warmth of her writhing body made the bandit immune to pain.

He stumbled over the silver hand, pitched drunkenly to the *k'ang* that ran along the wall. Velma's flailing legs kicked the opium lamp into a corner, extinguishing it. Hong Wu needed no light....

**FINALLY,** battered and half conscious, she sensed that he had ceased pawing her; though nothing now made any difference. She lay shuddering on the *k'ang*, and her misery reached its height when she realized that she had failed Bennett and her own vengeance. The intrusion of a vagrant moonbeam picked out the gleaming silver hand, that futile token of undying wrath.

Hong Wu was pulling noisily at a bottle whose pungent fumes filled the opium reeking room. She could just distinguish his bestial, pudgy face and tiny eyes. And as he wiped his gross lips, she prayed to a god unknown to her kindly father: Bennett's god of wrath.

For a moment she was strengthened as by a faint whisper and a stirring in the air about her; and the chill trickling down her spine was not the night air playing on her bruised and violated flesh. She shivered, feeling the presence of wonder beyond understanding; she was no longer alone with a brutal bandit, and her fate no longer horrified her.

Out of that evil darkness, an ever increasing concentration of life from beyond was strengthening her body and her courage. She began to understand, and she was glad for what had happened. There was still a chance.

She did not shrink when Hong Wu's flabby hands and gross mouth sought her in the dark. She did not repel him, even seemed to welcome his renewed attentions, even responded to his caresses. Her hands were busy—

Then she exclaimed, as though alarmed by some sound behind them. Hong Wu started; and as he turned his head and strained away from her a thick loop slipped over his throat: Velma's long hair, twisted and shaped into a running noose.

For an instant, he did not understand; and before he could yell, that soft, merciless hair had bitten deep into his throat. But though he was flabby and half drugged and entirely off guard, he was more than a match for his slender girlish enemy.

He clawed and struck and bit, bruising and tearing feminine flesh, but she clung to him like a snake, murder lust trebling her strength. He crushed her against the edge of the *k'ang*, fought the throttling strand, ripping and yanking until the agony made her head a roaring blaze of intolerable pain. But her battered, slender body clung to him like a tentacled vine, her lovely legs twined about his, her arms clutching, her thick hair choking, choking….

Her senses were swimming. The gods of wrath had forgotten her. But before blackness blotted out the wandering flashes of disjointed memories that marked the end of consciousness, the smoke that thickened the air and the dust motes stirred up by that silent, awful struggle seemed to take shape in the moonbeams that stole in through a single high window.

It was a hand—a monstrous, nebulous hand and wrist. Perhaps it was an hallucination, born of weakness, but she could have sworn it was a hand! Bennett's hand, interposing between her and Hong Wu. It was cold against her cheek and throat. It seemed to emerge from a whirling, solid darkness that the moon-glow could not penetrate; it was reaching from some dimension other than the three she knew. Its curving, taloned fingers twisted and curled, wraith-like around the fat, yellow neck....

Bennett was keeping his promise of vengeance, reaching from the grave... and Hong Wu's face showed an agony beyond any throttling. His eyes were bulging, and his tongue hung thickly from his gaping mouth. His head fell back heavily against the edge of the *k'ang*. There was a soft crunching. Velma, eyes closed from fear of the wonder before her face, knew that vertebrae were cracking from an inhuman unbearable torsion. And as she sank into a roaring, surging blackness, she felt cold lips against her cheeks and ear, but she could not understand the whispering....

*WHEN* Velma finally roused herself, every motion tore and pained her. Blood matted her streaming hair. Hong Wu lay face up, hideous and staring, his head wedged at an awful angle between the edge of the *k'ang* and the wall; his fingers still clutching the murderous black coil about his throat. His dying struggles had torn a part of the strand out by the roots.

She removed the noose, gathered her scattered garments. Something prompted her to lay the silver hand on Hong Wu's chest. It could have no further use to any one. Then she found his keys, and unlocked the inner door toward which she had vainly fled.

The camp was asleep, and sentries were readily eluded by her stealth.

When Velma reached Bennett's headquarters, the Northern Route Army was in confusion. Desertion and mutiny had followed when the news of the leader's death had finally leaked out. The officers were making half hearted attempts to rally the men. But this was nothing to Velma, as she stood in his tent, regarding that grim face which torture no longer distorted. Bennett was smiling, as though he had just kissed her.

"He died early in the evening," said the surgeon.

Velma nodded. "About two hours past moonrise, wasn't it?"

"How do you know?" he demanded.

"That," she said gravely, "was when he reached from the grave and throttled Hong Wu. Tell the Route Army to attack. A dead man will lead them to vengeance."

That night, she watched the red slaughter and was glad. But for a moment, her exultant smile became wistful, and she murmured, "If dad can see, maybe he knows why China converted me...."

Perhaps Bennett was explaining that to the deceased missionary. Though Velma tried to tell herself that, after all, it was possible that a long-haired woman could single handed have strangled Hong Wu.

COLBY QUINN

# hEARTS FROM thE hALF DEAD

*Two women harried him, and he decided
that one must die, if the other was to live and
give him her money. But there's more than
one slip to an experimental operation!*

**D**R. PHILIP GREER was probably too handsome, though he didn't think so. Hadn't his smooth good looks and charm snagged him a rich and beautiful wife? And didn't the old Don Juan stuff now enable him to break the simple hearts of little nurses and have his fun on the side?

In his arms at this moment was the latest little nurse to fall: Sally Myers, slender and brown-haired and young, and inexperienced enough to believe that Greer was God's right hand man.

It was in his private operating room, the doors were locked, and he was putting plenty of spirit into showing her that for him and her alone was the emotion of love invented and perpetuated unto this moment. Sally was breathing unsteadily and writhing reflexly as his touch inflamed her young and warm blood.

**SHE'D** been changing from her uniform to her dress when he came in, and she'd had on only sheer silk hose, step-ins and brassiere when he wrapped a knowing arm about her bare waist and pulled her close.

The new brassiere was of creamy lace, soft and transparent as her skin itself. Greer ran his fingers down along her spine like a ticklish feather and laughed at her spasmodic wriggle.

Her long and slender legs, silk-smooth and firm-muscled, trembled against his, and she moaned softly under his long kiss. When she pulled her mouth away gasping, she stood for a long moment with her head on his shoulder, eyes closed, feeling her skin twitch as his fingers traced patterns along her bare shoulders and arms.

"Sweetheart," she finally whispered, clasping her hands behind his neck, "when is it going to be? You keep telling me that soon you're going to get rid of her. How soon?—how soon can it be, so that we can be together all the time, without—well, hiding like this?"

Geer's teeth clicked almost inaudibly, against his will. "I keep telling you," he said, trying to cover with a show of irritation the finger of fear tapping him on the chest, "I keep telling you she'll drop off any day now. Just so I excite her enough…. Her heart's enlarging more and more and nothing can stop it. She knows it, though, and won't let herself get worked up… won't even let me make love to her any more." He felt the girl's fingers clutch his arm spasmodically. "But first," he finished with a shrug, "I've got to get her to change that damned will."

"To hell with that," the girl said impatiently. "I don't care about her money. I don't want it. What I want is you—not your wife's dough!"

"Well. I want it, all right." Greer said smoothly. "And we'll do it my way, honey. We can't live on love and shady operations."

The girl's lower lip drooped into a full, kissable pout, but Greer coolly let his arms fall from her. He looked at his wristwatch. "Well—"

"Oh, wait—please don't go!" Fear, a little unreasonable frenzy in her voice.

She caught his lapels and held him, letting the curve of her warm little breasts touch him through thin lacy covering. His coat was open and he could feel their pulsing roundnesses against his thin shirt.

Greer exhaled slowly, thoughtfully. She could get him all right. He admitted he couldn't keep away from her when she did things like this.

But he was getting a little afraid of her of late. What if she suddenly decided to go against him: got unreasonably jealous, for instance? What then? She knew too much, far too much, about his illegal surgery. She could make things tough, he knew. Best thing was to keep her in love with him until something happened. Something? Well, anything might happen to a girl in a doctor's office....

For a languid moment he watched the sway of her hips, white skin gleaming through the cream lace. Then he put his arms around her again, felt her skin, so tender, so sensitive, quiver beneath his touch.

"Don't worry, baby," he conceded with a quirking smile, "I'm not going yet."

*THE* other woman Philip Greer feared was his wife. She was twenty-nine and blonde and ravishingly beautiful; but she was cold to him.

"You know, sweetheart," she would warn when he got too eager, "you mustn't excite me, or my heart"—she would press her fingers to the base of one firm voluptuous breast—"my heart might give way, and then—well, darling, remember my will. You'd better," she would finish, sometimes harshly, "do your best to cure me!"

"But I tell you," groaned her husband, often enough and sincerely at such times, "I do do my best. What the hell you think I'm doing—giving you slow poison? Enlarged heart! Honey, it kills me to think of it, but there's nothing you can do for that except take it easy.... Trouble is, we don't know what causes a heart to enlarge, and hence we don't have a cure. Please, as you love me, don't hold *me* responsible for an act of God!"

"Act of God," she answered. "Yeah, I know! You're just wanting me to die so you can get hold of my money and start playing around with other women—if," she added suspiciously, "you haven't already started."

He sighed at such moments, as if in despair at the innate unreasonableness of woman. "My will," her relentless voice continued, so often that he heard it in his sleep, "provides that if I die within the next ten years, *you get not one cent of my money.* Not a penny, do you hear?"

Philip Greer heard, all right. He couldn't help it. Not, he admitted to himself, that he would have cared particularly if she died the next day—if only it hadn't been for that will. As long as she lived she gave him a more than generous allowance, and she was intensely infatuated with him (though a hell of a lot of good it did him!).

Somehow, he had to try to keep her alive for the sake of her money; as for women—well he had plenty of them, even if she didn't know it. But he didn't want to lose her money.

But God knew how you could cure an enlarged heart that was getting worse all the time! She'd be kicking off any month now, and nothing could convince her it wasn't all his fault—that he wasn't giving her some mysterious poison to get rid of her.

*AFTER* he left Sally in his operating room, Greer pounced into his coupe and started for home. He stopped at the corner newsstand to get the evening paper and paused with the paper before him on the steering wheel for a brief glance at the news. A boxed item in the middle of page one caught and held his eye. Then his heart began bounding. The article read;

### TRANSFERS LIVING HEARTS

The successful transfer of a living heart from one dog's body to another was described today. Dr. Daniel Thurston, young local medical research worker, gave the statement to reporters from his experimental laboratory.

"I started out with fish," he explained. "Then I worked on guinea pigs, and then on dogs…. The hearts stop beating, of course, during the operation, I start them pumping again with a stimulant. That nearly always works—you may know that the hearts of dead persons have often been revived to normal cardiac function by stimulants—even several hours after death.

"The hearts slow down a little at first, but after a few minutes they pick up to normal. I'm working on a better method," he added, "whereby an artificial heart—a glass pump—keeps the blood circulating during the operation."

When asked if an exchange of hearts could be successfully performed on human beings, Dr. Thurston only laughed. "Why," he asked, "would anyone want to do that?"

But Philip Greer knew why! He felt faint merely thinking of the possibilities. If he had to keep his rich and beautiful wife alive,

and couldn't do anything to cure her diseased heart—then why not give her a new one?

The thought of where he would get the new, strong heart didn't bother him then. Perhaps he had Sally Myers in the back of his mind; or perhaps he didn't think of her until she suddenly stuck her curly brown head through the car's open window and laughed merrily.

"Hello!"

"What is it?" he growled. His eyes narrowed and his little moustache twitched. He didn't like people to see him on the street with his nurse.

"I followed you in a taxi," she explained. "Because—well, because I forgot something when you were there."

"What?" he asked suspiciously.

"I need some money."

"The hell! I just gave you fifty bucks, day before yesterday. What kind of salary do you think you draw, anyway?"

*They found her with
the knife in one hand,
the gun beside her.*

"Now, honey, don't be mean," she coaxed, her tone confident, knowing. "This isn't salary, anyway. It's friendly consideration… and we're friends, aren't we?"

Greer swore inwardly. The girl knew too much about him. It was blackmail, that's what it was!

"How much do you want?" he asked coldly.

"Another fifty will do for the time being," she said.

Greer glanced hastily around. No one he knew was passing. Quickly he gave her the money in bills.

"You're sweet!" She threw him a little kiss.

How high-handed she was, digging him like this, he thought; yet how pleading when it came to love! He caught her hand; felt her return the pressure.

"You know I don't mind giving you money," he lied smoothly.

"Loving you the way I do.... By the way, want to meet me in the operating room tonight?"

She laughed. "I'll be there." With a quick squeeze of his fingers, she left him.

Greer watched her walk away, trim calves flashing youth. "She'll do," he muttered. "Strong as a young ox, and same class blood donor, too.... There'd have to be *some* blood transfused in the heart itself...."

He could feed her a knockout drop and give her ether and she'd never know what had happened to her. Getting rid of the body would be easy.

He'd better tell his wife what was going on, though, he decided.

*SHE* was reading on a chaise lounge in her boudoir and frowned when Greer came in.

"Can't you knock?" She made as if to pull the thin negligee over her thighs, but when he came over beside her, her long, shapely legs were still exposed—almost their full length. Clenching his fists, he could almost *hear* the tender skin of her thighs swishing one against the other as she crossed her knees.

Anna smiled malevolently and stretched her arms upward so that he would have to watch the slip-slide of her youthful, breasts beneath the sheer chiffon of her negligee.

She ached for him sometimes... yearned to have him hold her and caress her as he had at first; but fear—the twisted fear of death—superseded all else and held her back.

Greer relaxed after a moment and laughed shortly. "No time for that hooey now, darling," he said smoothly; "I know it gives you a kick to tease me. And it's a second-hand thrill, if you ask me.... But here's what! I've discovered a cure for your heart!"

"Philip!" Anna leaned toward him, then clapped her hand to her breast and dropped back, breathing heavily. "It's too exciting for me, just hearing you say that. What—what have you discovered?"

He led up to it gradually; then told her. "It's your only chance," he finished huffily. "Money or not, you can't live as you are. Nobody can cure the heart yon have, but now I can get you a new one.

"Where'll you get the new one?"

"Leave that to me."

Her eyes closed to slits, but she smiled thinly. "I'll trust you, Philip, darling; for, remember, my will still holds good—and for *your* dear sake this operation'd better be a success."

**DR. DAN THURSTON** buttoned his topcoat and belted it around him, glancing at the starless sky. He'd worked late and would be glad of a few hours sleep.

But as he opened the car door, a gun was jammed into his kidneys and a figure he'd been vaguely aware of preceding down the street caught him by the shoulder and turned him around.

"Get in," said the man. "I'll go with you."

"Greer!" Thurston recognized the man with astonishment. "What the hell's this?" he growled, trying to shove the gun away. But Greer only jammed the muzzle hard into his belly and said coldly:

"Sure, it's Greer. I don't care if you recognize me. Because I just want you to do me a favor. You're going to perform an operation on my wife—to save her life."

Thurston clapped him on the shoulder. "Put your gun away and don't be silly," he said sympathetically. "You don't need a gun to make me operate to save a life. I know it's your wife and you're all wrought up, but…"

Greer sighed and put the gun in his pocket, still watching Thurston narrowly, however.

"Thanks, old man," he muttered. "Guess I *am* a little on edge."

*SO* he didn't tell Thurston what was what until they stood in the operating room and Greer had locked the door. His finger curled over the trigger of the gun in his pocket.

"*Two* of them?" cried Thurston.

There were two operating tables close together, and on each was the stripped form of a woman, covered by a sheet. He whirled on Greer, looked down the barrel of the latter's automatic.

"Yes, two of them," Greer said quietly. "Here's your chance: from fish to guinea pigs to dogs to humans. You're going to trans-

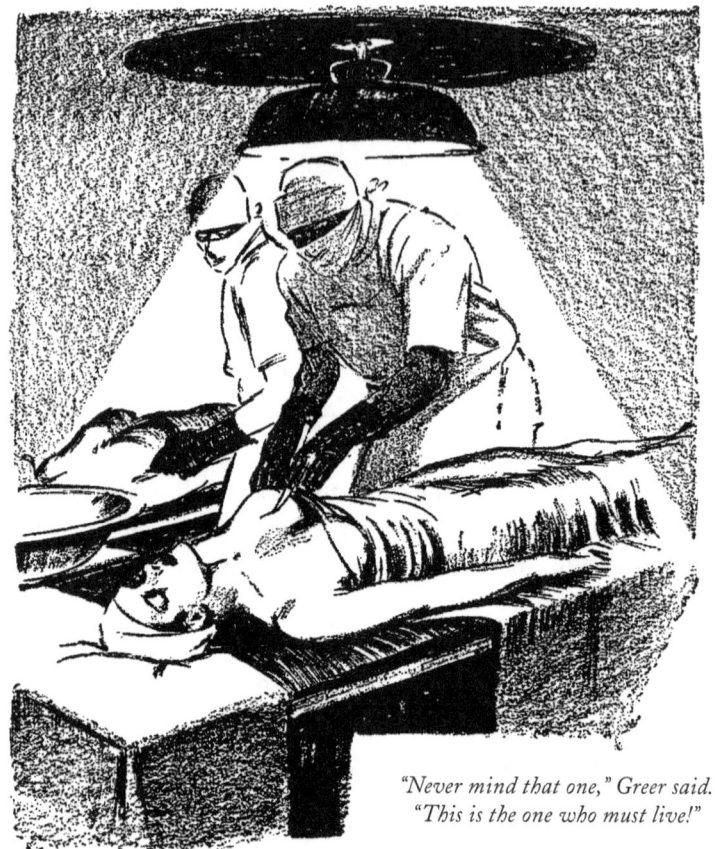

*"Never mind that one," Greer said.
"This is the one who must live!"*

fer the hearts of these two subjects. This one"—he pointed to
Sally Myers—"you don't have to bother with. But this one"—he
indicated his wife—"must live. If she does, you leave here alive.
If she doesn't—"

"What if I refuse?" Thurston asked coolly.

"In that case, being a friend of yours, I'll yield to an emer-
gency and investigate the pain which you think is appendicitis. I
shall faint while you're under the ether, however, and by the time
I recover and call the coroner, I'll be too late to keep you from
bleeding to death...."

"You'd have a good chance of hanging for it," Thurston said
quietly. Then he shrugged. "Where are your instruments. You
must help me, you know. I can't do it alone."

"I know."

They went to work. Thurston didn't have to ask why when he opened Anna's chest cavity and saw the size of her heart. He shook his head. But his hands sped on, deftly. Behind the gauze, his lips moved, clipped out orders to Greer.

And Greer was doing his best. Envy flooded him when he thought of his own position and of what this other man had achieved, so young....

"Wait, damn you!" Greer gritted a minute later. "Leave her alone. *Here's* the one!"

For Thurston was working over Sally Myers' body—body it was, with its heart out and its blood a still stream without the pulse of life.

Thurston didn't even look up.

"Be quiet!" he snapped. "I hold the upper hand now. We finish this one first or we don't go on at all."

Greer subsided. Sweat popped out on his face as arteries were skillfully connected with dissolvable suture. Anna's pitifully enlarged heart crowded Sally's unbreathing lungs.

"The adrenalin!" snapped Thurston, with the final stitch closing the chest cavity.

He made the injection. More. There was a twitch, a frightening jump inside her chest, a surge—and blood was pumping.

Thurston wheeled to Anna's lifeless body, took the bloody heart of Sally from the basin. This heart was stronger: it could better stand delay than the other one....

And while working over the lovely form of Sally, Dan Thurston had known a sudden longing for her to live, even with a diseased heart.

Minutes later both women were breathing; Anna steadily, Sally in long, wavering gusts. Her pulse, too, was slower than the other; jumpy and irregular; and Thurston spent his time over her, ready to stimulate her to the point of death if necessary.

"They'll both live," Thurston told Greer a couple of hours later. "Now tell me why I shouldn't have you sent to prison."

"Because you can't prove anything."

"No," Thurston said, "that's not the reason. I could prove plenty.... I think. I'm going to leave you alone because you're going to let me take this girl away from here and see that she gets well. Somehow I think that if I left her here, my operation might become a failure."

Greer turned pale.

"What did you tell her?" Thurston asked.

"I—I examined her and told her she had an ulcer of the stomach—and I'd have to operate. I gave her ether, and that's all."

"I'll take care of the rest." Thurston smiled quizzically. "Good luck with your patient."

**DAN THURSTON** had plenty good luck with *his* patient. Two months later he was still making her sit in a wheel chair. But as he looked up from two X-Ray negatives he'd been examining against the window, he said exultantly: "Your heart's strong enough to stand kissing me now!"

And Sally stood up and walked over to him and put her arms about him simply. She'd never felt *this* way about Philip Greer! Sally didn't even know she had a new heart. Dan had told her it was weak, though, from the operation he'd performed in Greer's place.

Thurston glanced at the negatives again. The size of her heart had reduced noticeably since he'd transferred it from Anna Greer's body—and would, he was sure, shrink to normal size. If nobody knew what caused hearts to enlarge, how could they be so sure—as Greer had—that the trouble lay in the heart itself? Apparently it didn't. And so Thurston knew what must be happening to Anna Greer....

**PHILIP GREER** knew too. Anna stepped down from the platform of the chest-fluoroscope and Philip turned pale at what he had just seen. Her heart was enlarging day by day! Soon it would be as large as before. The operation—all the risk he'd taken—had been for nothing!

"It's all right!" he assured her heartily. "You're coming along swell!"

"I'm so glad," she murmured. "Because now I can love you again."

She came close to him and twined her arms about his neck. She hugged herself close to him.

"The way my heart pounds," she murmured, breathing in gasps, "the way it pounds for you—feels almost as it did when—when—"

She clutched her heart agonizedly and dropped to the floor. Greer picked her up and carried her to the couch. Blood was seeping through her blouse, and he knew the incision had opened.

He rushed from the room. When he returned, moments later, with a kit, Anna had regained consciousness. Not only that: she had a pistol and she had her finger tight on the trigger.

"Damn you!" she gasped. "You're poisoning me again. It was all a blind! I'll show you about heart-transferring!"

The little gun didn't make much noise, and neither did Philip Greer: for the bullet clipped neatly through the right wing of his mustache and passed through the back of his brain.

They found him with his chest opened and his heart ripped out; and his wife dead beside him; in one hand his torn heart, in the other a bloody scalpel. They said she'd died of heart failure....

# hELL'S DARK FRAGRANCE

*Over the perfume factory an evil blight had fallen.*
*One after another the girls developed a strange illness,*
*turning rich red blood to a dirty green, changing*
*feminine loveliness to unspeakable loathsomeness.*

*IN THE* bitter January night, Geoffrey Harde shivered. Icy knives of wind sliced through his flesh, and the road's frozen ruts were daggers under the worn soles of his shoes as he trudged wearily through the woods toward his cousin's somber house.

Yet the shudder which touched Geoffrey Harde's shoulders was not entirely due to the wind's penetrating fingers thrusting through his threadbare coat. There was something in the night's frigid stillness that stirred vague premonitions within him—

It was an inexplicable feeling deep in the recesses of his sub-consciousness. Somehow it seemed to be linked with his cousin, the dark and saturnine Adam Allister, who had written a letter inviting him here; who had promised him a job. There had been something odd about Allister's letter; something vaguely wrong. Or was it all just imagination?

On either side of the road, the denuded trees stretched out skeletal limbs like grotesque supplicants praying to some dark unholy god. On the ground, the wind stirred through dead leaves with tiny slither noises. Even the distant stars seemed baleful. Again Geoffrey Harde shivered.

*AT* last he neared his cousin's Colonial mansion. It lay beyond the margin of the grove, and it was more than just a house; for behind the dwelling a darker, vaster structure loomed. This was the building where Adam Allister's perfumes were distilled, bottled; where the girl employees of the plant lived and had their sleeping quarters on the floor above.

Abruptly, as Geoffrey drew close to the mansion and the darkened factory behind it, he tensed. From somewhere in the distance there came a shrill, maniacal scream!

It was a sound that seemed to be torn from the throat of hell itself; the wail of a soul plunging into stark, abysmal terror. It was a woman's rasping, keening, horrified cry!

Geoffrey stared ahead. Toward him through the night he saw a wraith-like figure racing.

It was a girl! A naked girl!

Her hair streamed out behind her and her legs flashed white as she ran. Her breasts were quivering globes of flesh, undulating with each frantic stride; and as she sped onward toward Geoffrey Harde, she uttered another blood-congealing scream.

"What the devil!" he rasped; and he sprang toward the running girl. Even as he leaped into her path he beheld another figure desperately pursuing her. This second form was another woman—a young woman with raven hair and lush, mature figure. A thin *robe de nuit* clung silkily to her as she ran, outlining the rounded nubility of her body.

Suddenly the first girl—the nude one—plummeted into Goeffrey's outstretched arms. As he caught her, she moaned and collapsed against him. Unwittingly his palms touched her bare skin; and his fingers subconsciously detected a myriad of rough irregularities upon the smoothness of her death-cold flesh, like pitted holes or tiny sores, raw, open, bleeding.

He held her, tried to steady her, but she was a limp weight in his arms. He peered into her face; saw that her cheeks were etiolated, bloodless; saw that her eyes were wide and staring and glazing.

A premonition inched worm-like through Geoffrey's veins. He pressed his hand over the girl's heart, sank his fingers into the pitted flesh under her rounded left breast—

"God!" he whispered bewilderedly. *"She's dead!"*

It was true. There was no flicker of heartbeat. The girl had died in his arms! Fear-syncope—or something more foul and more sinister—had slain her!

**UNBELIEVINGLY,** Geoffrey once again felt for some faint heartbeat; but there was none. He drew his hand away and noticed that his palm was sticky with some wet, slimy, viscid substance. At first he thought it was blood; but when he looked to make sure, a sudden wave of revulsion churned frothily in his belly.

*The viscid substance was green!*

In horror he stared at the dead girl's breasts. They gleamed pallidly in the darkness, like two rounded mounds of snowy

*The weight bashed full into the back of the hooded figure.*

marble. But upon each bared breast, Geoffrey now perceived hundreds of minute punctures pitted into the flesh—

And from each puncture, turgid green slime suppurated!

"God!" Geoffrey Harde rasped. "Her blood—*it's turned green!*"

In sudden repugnance he dropped the corpse; allowed it to slump in a macabre sprawl at his feet What foul thing was this, that turned human corpuscles from ruby to slimy emerald?

Then Geoffrey remembered the second girl who had come running towards the woods—the raven-haired, voluptuous one in the silken nightgown. Momentarily he had forgotten her, but now he remembered. He turned, searched for her with his narrowed eyes. Suddenly he spotted her. She was hovering nervously near the edge of the barren grove. White-faced, she was staring back at him.

Dimly he perceived the lush outlines of her perfect body, the swelling domes of her breasts, the lyric arches of her hips through her single gossamer garment. Her face held a tense beauty; but

either in imagination or by some trick of the frozen starlight, Geoffrey thought he detected a malign glitter in her dark eyes...

He leaped toward her. "You!" he rasped. "This girl's dead—and you were chasing her! I want an explanation—"

Before he could utter another word, the brunette turned, darted into the grove, vanished like a flitting specter.

Geoffrey Harde cursed in his throat. She knew something! She was connected in some fashion with the naked girl's death! If must be true—else why had she pursued the unclad one? And why did she now plunge into the grove to escape questioning?

With a snarl, Geoffrey leaped after her. He went smashing into the sinister woods, hurled himself into the dark morass of frozen shadows. But he caught no glimpse of his quarry. It was as if the frigid earth had opened and swallowed her.

*TWICE* he stopped in his tracks to listen, hoping to catch some sound of her progress; but only mocking silence rewarded him. At last he knew that she had eluded him; that he could not hope to trace her in the tangled darkness of the denuded glade. He must retrace his steps, get back to the road. He must reach the mansion of his cousin, Adam Allister, and turn in an alarm. He must tell of the girl who had died in his arms...

Grimly he fought his way out of the grove, came to the nude feminine corpse. He leaned over the body, gently straightened it. And as he leaned over the dead girl, there came to his nostrils a strange, weird fragrance. The cloying odor seemed to emanate from the corpse itself; and it held a macabre, intoxicating, flower-like redolence at once fascinating and yet noxious. Somehow it reminded Geoffrey of passion... and of death...

He whipped off his threadbare topcoat, spread it over the dead girl. Then he sped toward Allister's house.

He gained the Colonial porch. With frantic grimness he lifted the brass knocker, pounded it. He could hear the echoes resounding hollowly within the tomb-like reaches of the mansion; but for a long time he got no other response.

Once more he pounded the knocker. And then, unexpectedly, the door opened in his face.

Geoffrey Harde stared into the azure eyes of a tall, willowy, yellow-haired woman—a woman whose negligee was of such gossamer texture that he could discern every line of the cones of her unbrassiered breasts and the slender, sylph-like symmetry of her hips and her columnar thighs. Beneath the negligee she wore utterly nothing; and the sight of her feminine, nubile curves filled Geoffrey with a sudden electrical sensation.

It was not only the revelation of her sweet, intimate curves that caused his heart to leap. It was something else. It was the fact that he recognized her—

"Alycia! Alycia Maddern!" he whispered in astonishment.

"You—Geoffrey!" she answered. And she held out her arms.

He swept her into his embrace, crushed her against him until he could feel her firm breasts being flattened upon his chest. And why should he not thus hold Alycia Maddern? Once he had been engaged to her, long years ago...

*FIVE* years. Five eternities, rather! That had been before Geoffrey Harde's uncle had died; when Geoffrey had expected one day to inherit a half share of his uncle's estate. But when the old man had died, Geoffrey found himself disinherited. His uncle's fortune and perfume business had all gone to Harde's cousin, the swarthy and saturnine Adam Allister.

And so, with no prospects, Geoffrey had relinquished Alycia; had broken their engagement, gone away. But now... the intervening five years faded and vanished. Once more he was holding Alycia in his arms.

"Alycia!" he murmured again. "Alycia!" And he kissed her on the lips, held her close...

She drew back from him. "No, Geoffrey. I'm not the Alycia Maddern you know. I am Alycia Allister now."

"You mean—you married my cousin?"

"Yes, Geoffrey."

His momentary pang of regret was not as sharp as he might have expected. "You—you've been happy?" he asked her quietly.

She cast him an odd, sidelong glance; did not directly answer his question. Instead, she murmured: "I—I wanted you to come back here, Geoffrey. That's why I persuaded Adam to offer you a job in the perfume factory. After all, you're his only relative. And he's very wealthy now. He invented a new perfume formula; a fragrance that sells like wildfire. He calls it *Parfum l'Enfer*—fragrance of hell. And it's well-named, Geoffrey! It's a subtle, intoxicating stuff; it's made us rich. Why shouldn't you share some of Adam's good fortune?"

As she mentioned Adam Allister's new creation, *Parfum l'Enfer*, Geoffrey suddenly remembered why he had come running so desperately here to his cousin's house. He remembered the girl who had died in his arms, back by the grove.

To his nostrils there now came a recollection of that fragrance which seemingly had emanated from the dead girl's flesh. It had

*Something bludgeoned down on Geoffrey's unprotected head.*

been cloying, yet noxiously hellish. *Parfum l'Enfer*—fragrance of hell! That must have been the odor which had clung to the feminine corpse!

Geoffrey Harde stared into Alycia's azure eyes. "Listen!" he rasped out. "Where is Adam Allister? I must see him—now!"

She gave him a worried look. "Y-you can't see him now, Geoffrey. Adam has been ill; he had a breakdown from overwork and worry and nervous strain. The doctor gave him some sleeping tablets this evening. We can't disturb him. It might—"

"But we must! We've got to disturb him! This is damned serious!"

"Why—wh-what do you mean, Geoffrey?"

He lowered his voice. "Alycia," he said tensely, "as I was coming toward your house just now a girl ran toward me. She was stark naked! I caught her in my arms—and she died as I held her! And her breasts were pitted with hundreds of open sores; *her blood had turned green!*"

Alycia went death-pale. "Oh, God! Another one!" she moaned. Abruptly she collapsed into Geoffrey's arms, clung to him. Her body shook with convulsive shudders, and he could feel the wild hammering of her heart upon his chest.

He stared into her eyes. *"Another* one?" he rasped. "What do you mean by that?"

**SHE** fused herself against him as if seeking the protection of his muscular, sinewy body. "Geoffrey—it's a strange, terrible blight that's fallen on us! Several of our factory girls have developed those pitted green sores on their b-breasts…. We've had doctors out here, but none seemed able to diagnose what's wrong. And now… you say one of the girls… is dead…!"

"Yes! I left her corpse by the grove. We've got to bring it here to the house, notify an undertaker." Geoffrey's mouth was a grim line. "Alycia, I have a feeling that this thing that turns human blood from red to green slime is something evil—something beyond ordinary medicine. Perhaps it's a poison! The police must be notified, Alycia; an investigation started!"

"Y-yes. That's what I wanted to do from the very first; but

Adam wouldn't listen to me. Instead, he worried himself into a breakdown…" She disengaged herself from Geoffrey's embrace. "Wait here until I get a coat. Then we'll go and get that c-corpse…!"

She was gone a brief moment; then she returned, clad in a long coat. Geoffrey took her hand, led her quickly across the frozen clearing to the grove's edge. He went to the spot where he had left the dead girl; and suddenly, festering maggots of nameless dread slithered through his veins.

"God!" he whispered. "The corpse—*it's gone!*"

Alycia swayed unsteadily. "Geoffrey! How could such a thing happen? Are you sure she was dead?"

"I'm positive!" he answered grimly. "There's something hellish, diabolic, about all this! We've got to phone the police!"

He sped back toward the looming, ominously-dark house, with the golden-haired Alycia racing beside him. They entered the mansion, went into a front room. Geoffrey snatched up the telephone, clattered the receiver hook. A dark scowl crossed his face.

"The line's dead!" he whispered. "*Somebody cut the wires!*"

The girl's face drained of all color. "Oh, God!" she moaned. There was terror in her eyes; abysmal fear.

Geoffrey whirled to her. "Have you a car here? I'm going to drive back to the city for the police!"

"Y-yes. There's a car. But—but please don't leave me, Geoffrey! I'm afraid! Something sinister is in the very air! I—I'm frightened!"

"Then come with me."

"I—I can't leave Adam alone, Geoffrey. He's asleep; he's had sleeping medicine. I can't leave him. Oh, Geoffrey—don't go back to town tonight! Stay here with me until daylight…!"

Geoffrey started to refuse her; and she must have read the negation in his eyes, for slowly her clenched hand opened, her hand that had clutched her negligee so tightly about her lithe body, allowed the sleazy garment to slip down half off her shoulders revealing a tempting area of warm, palpitating flesh.

Like a glorious goddess she stood there; permitted his eyes to drink in the lilting contours of her body, the soft but firm hillocks of her breasts.

"Geoffrey!" she whispered frantically. "Stay here with me! Please—please! Stay, and I'll see that you won't be sorry!"

He felt some of the old, long-forgotten thrill beginning to course through him. The years had not dimmed the glory of her figure, the beauty of her flesh. And she was practically offering herself, if he would stay in the house with her! In her fear of being alone, she was offering... everything!

Yet he remembered that other girl—the one who had died in his arms out there in the frigid night. He remembered her limp, pathetic body; the green-festering sores that disfigured her young breasts... Something horrible, ghastly, inhuman, had done that to her. Something malignant, demoniac, which must be ferreted out, discovered, destroyed...

Something which must be destroyed before it could work further harm to the girl employees of the perfume factory; to Alycia Allister herself....

GRIMLY, Geoffrey Harde shook his head. "No, Alycia. I can't stay. I've got to drive to town for the police. And we must find the corpse of that girl who died. We must find the fiendish thing that killed her!"

"Geoffrey—you can't leave me!" Alycia whispered frantically. And she came to him, her body trembling, desperately clinging to him.

The touch of her flesh ignited an inner searing flame that melted his resolve. And as her lips met his mouth he knew that he must stay here in this house until morning... He must stay and protect her, because she trusted him...

"I'll stay!" he whispered.

Then, suddenly, from somewhere upstairs came a muffled groan, like the weird and hollow plaint of an ungraved ghost!

Alycia leaped back. *"What was that?"* she panted.

Geoffrey grabbed at her. "Could it be Adam, moaning in his sleep?"

"No! It couldn't be—!"

"Then we'll go see what it was!" he grated. Together they raced upstairs. Alycia led Geoffrey to a closed bedroom door. She opened it, snapped on the lights within the room. Harde saw his dark and swarthy cousin lying upon the bed.

Swiftly, Alycia crossed the room; leaned over her husband. Then she straightened. "He's all right," she whispered. "His heart is beating normally. Come, before we disturb him!" She returned to Geoffrey, led him out of the room, snapped off the light and closed the door behind her.

Then she took Harde to another room down the hallway. "You can stay h-here tonight, Geoffrey," she faltered.

"Thank you."

"And—and if anything frightens me, you w-won't object if I come in?"

He felt the heat of her glance, the nearness of her lovely body. He thought he understood what she meant: that she would return to him later for the comfort of his arms…

In imagination he envisioned himself holding her, caressing her, kissing her lips… But she was his cousin's wife, now. He dared not think of her in any other way…

*SHE* left him alone in the little guest bedroom; and when she had gone, he locked the door. Then he turned off the lights; stretched himself, still fully dressed, across the bed. He attuned his ears to the minor sounds of the night. If that groan came again, he must leap into action—

Suddenly, he heard a noise in the solid darkness of his room.

He crouched, and soundlessly, he waited. To his nostrils drifted a sudden fragrance—cloying, heady, funereal. He recognized it. *Parfum l'Enfer!* Fragrance of hell! The fragrance which had clung to the corpse of the girl who had died in his arms…!

In the blackness of that chamber, sweat stood out in cold globules on Geoffrey's forehead. That dead girl's body had vanished as if into thin air. And now… he pictured the nude, undead thing creeping toward him…

"God!" he whispered. He fumbled in a pocket, found a match, flared it on his thumbnail. He stared.

*White-faced, the other girl hovered there, watching. In sudden repugnance Geoffrey turned from the girl he was holding.*

There came the sound of a sharp, indrawn breath. Then, as Geoffrey's eyes became accustomed to the flickering light, he saw someone coming toward him—

It was the lush, voluptuous, brunette girl he had seen at the edge of the grove! The one he had pursued into the woods, only to lose her.

"You!" he barked. He dropped the match, sprang at her.

She tried to avoid him, but his hands closed on her shoulders. She struggled. Her thin night gown ripped. As he clutched her in a crushing embrace he could feel the resilient, warm mounds of her breasts jabbing his chest; could hear her labored breathing, her frightened gasps.

"You don't get away this time!" he gritted. He tripped her. She went down, squirming. In the darkness he pinioned her with the weight of his own hard body. And as he felt her struggles growing weaker beneath him, he was suddenly aware of a strange, new sensation within his veins—a flooding riptide of emotion, more animal than human, at the nearness and helplessness of his feminine victim.

Yet over this atavistic urge which now possessed him, his cold reason still functioned. This was the girl who had pursued that dying young woman across the open space outside the house. She knew the answer to the riddle of the dead girl's lacerated breasts and green-slimed blood.

*HE* pinned her to the floor. "I've got you now!" he growled out savagely. "I've got you, and I'm going to make you talk. You're going to tell me what you know about that girl who died in my arms! You're going to tell me why you were running after her!"

"I—I can't—"

"You'll tell me! Either you'll talk, or... you'll wish you had!"

"No! D-don't hurt me! I—" the girl's voice was a strangled, terror-laden whisper in the blackness of the room.

"I've something else in mind besides hurting you!" Geoffrey rasped. And he fumbled, in the darkness, toward her.

She gasped as his clutching fingers dug into the soft flesh of her shoulders. She struggled as his hands slid down the delicious roundness of her arms. He crushed his mouth bruisingly against hers, forcing her lips open with savage impetuousness. And then his kisses wandered downward toward the throbbing hollow of her warm throat...

"You'll talk, or I'll—" Geoffrey Harde permitted the sentence to go unfinished; but his voice was freighted with grim passionate meaning.

"Oh, God!" the girl moaned. "I—I'll tell everything I know, if you—you'll stop—"

"Then start talking!"

"I—I intended to tell you everything, anyhow!" she whispered tremblingly. "That was why I came here to your room! I—I hoped that you'd listen to me and help me…!"

"Help you?" Geoffrey demanded.

"Yes, help me. When I heard you downstairs, talking to Mrs. Allister, I realized that you couldn't be involved in the hellish things that are going on here. Your very words—your desire to go after the police—proved to me that you were innocent…"

Geoffrey stiffened in the darkness. "I? Innocent? Innocent of what?"

"Innocent of helping your cousin, Adam Allister, in his fiendish work!" the girl answered. Then her words tumbled out in swift coherence. "Listen! Adam Allister's illness is a fake, a sham. He pretends to be sick in order to fool his wife and give himself an alibi. At least, that's the way I think it is. But I believe that actually Allister is the one who killed that girl who died in your arms tonight! I believe he's feeding some deadly poison to the girls who work in his perfume plant!"

Geoffrey released the brunette girl; helped her to her feet in the darkness of the room. He drew her toward himself, steadied her by slipping an arm about her pliant waist. The intimate contact thrilled him queerly; sent racing tingles through his pulse. It was queer, but this girl's nearness stirred him far more than the nearness of the yellow-haired Alycia, whom he had loved in the old days…

*HE* held the brunette girl close to him. "Tell me everything!" he demanded in a sharp whisper. "Start from the beginning!"

"I—I'm not sure of anything," she faltered. "I just came here recently, got a job in Adam Allister's perfume factory. My name is Myrna Campbell; I'm a newspaper woman. My paper got wind of the mysterious disease which has been attacking the girls in Allister's plant; I was sent here to investigate. I found out that the girl employees sleep in small, individual rooms over the factory, ostensibly because the plant is located so far from town. And I've discovered that there is something queer about the way those girls sleep at night. It's as if they were drugged; as if they were fed some narcotic in their evening meal. They sleep almost as if they were d-dead!"

"Go on!" Geoffrey pressed her arm.

"In the morning, the girls awaken with strange sores on their breasts. They are weak, listless. I think it's the poison they're being fed. And I think Adam Allister is doing it!"

"But why? Why, in God's name?"

"I—I don't know!" she answered.

Geoffrey pursued his inquisition. "What about tonight? Who was the girl who ran naked into my arms, and then died?"

"She was a factory worker. I heard her screaming. I hadn't eaten my own supper tonight, so I was not drugged, not asleep. I heard her screaming; I jumped out of bed and saw her running across the clearing. I followed her. At first, when you grabbed her, I thought you were one of Allister's helpers. That's why I ran from you. I hid in the woods until you went away. When you had gone, I took the dead girl's body and hid it in the grove. I intended to take it to the city tomorrow for an autopsy."

"And why are you in my room now?"

"I slipped into the house to see what I might discover about you. When I heard you talking to Mrs. Allister, I knew you weren't mixed up in what has been going on here. I groaned to make you come upstairs; then I hid in this room, in the closet. I wanted to wait until you were alone, so that I could talk to you."

"And that perfume you're wearing." Geoffrey Harde whispered, "it's *Parfum l'Enfer*, isn't it? It clings to you because you work in the stuff?"

"Y-yes."

He drew her even closer. "Listen, Myrna. You and I are going to conduct a quiet investigation right now. And if my cousin is guilty of the things you suspect, we'll turn him over to the po—"

Before Geoffrey could complete the sentence, he heard a sound behind him. Someone had entered the room. Out of the blackness a harsh voice snarled: "You'll do nothing, Cousin Geoffrey—*except die!*"

And then something bludgeoned down on Geoffrey's unprotected skull. He felt the bruising, brain-shattering impact of a cudgel, a blackjack. Agony lanced through his mind, his soul. He heard the voluptuous, brunette Myrna Campbell cry out in deadly terror. And then... nothingness....

*CONSCIOUSNESS* returned to Geoffrey to the accompaniment of a raging inferno of pain in his temples. He tried to move; and then came the sickening realization that his wrists were handcuffed behind him, and his ankles fettered to some heavy iron weight by means of a length of chain.

A dim light burned overhead. In its yellow glow, he saw that he was in an underground cavern—a subterranean chamber hewn out of the living earth. The fetid reek of dampness was upon the hell-hot air; and with it drifted a weird, overpowering fragrance.

Geoffrey's eyes traversed the four sides of the huge underground chamber. He drew a sharp breath as he saw the source of the cloying perfume—

This chamber was a subterranean hothouse! A place for the growing of strange, exotic, blossoming plants! Pallidly colorless, the blooms depended from row after row of thick green stalks rising out of the dank earth; and from each stalk, countless tendrils extended, like octopus arms dripping with green chlorophyll.

Under each plant, Geoffrey saw a small pan designed to catch the emerald chlorophyll exudation as it dripped from the extended tendrils. Abruptly, he realized that it must be this slimy green matter which went into the production of his cousin's hellish perfume—*Parfum l'Enfer*. And there was something sinister in the very appearance of the blossoms. In texture and coloring they resembled putrescent flesh...

Suddenly, Geoffrey heard a sound. It was the whirring of a hidden, powerful motor. Then he noticed a door set into one wall of the subterranean chamber. As he looked, the door slid open.

It was an elevator shaft!

Slowly a platform descended into view. Geoffrey narrowed his eyes to mere slits, pretended still to be unconscious. The elevator-platform reached the floor level of the cellar. It stopped. A figure shrouded in black from head to foot stepped from the platform. Hooded, masked, the black-shrouded shape wheeled out an object resembling an oversized operating table on rubber-tired rollers. And upon that table lay three unconscious, semi-nude girls!

Geoffrey saw the black-shrouded figure drag the three senseless girls from the wheeled table, one at a time. He saw the unconscious girls being tugged toward one particular row of pallid-blossomed plants. And then—

The sheer, unadulterated, fiendish horror that happened next was like a mind-shattering unreality, a phantasmagoria of impossible viciousness. The three unconscious girls were dumped at the roots of the row of plants. Then, like a devil's miracle, an unutterable thing happened.

*The green tendrils growing out of the thick stalks started swaying, moving, like octopus arms suddenly come alive!*

They moved—downward!

Like seeking, hungry tentacles, they snaked toward the nude torsos of the three unconscious girls. Then, ultimate of horrors, the nodule-suckers at the ends of the tendrils fastened upon living, breathing human flesh!

Fastened… battened… and punctured with a myriad of vegetable mouths of spike-sharp keenness!

And now Geoffrey Harde understood the real truth at last. This was how Adam Allister created his hellish new fragrance, *Parfum l'Enfer!* Fragrance of hell! The stuff was well-named! *Because it was distilled from flowers that feasted on living human blood!*

**TO** keep his flowers alive, Allister must have drugged his girl employees at night with some hypnotic opiate. That was Allister's true reason for insisting that his girl factory hands must live over the factory itself. And when the girls were drugged, unconscious, they were brought down here to this subterranean chamber of horrors. They were brought here so that the carnivorous green plant tendrils could drink warm, flowing blood from snowy feminine breasts…!

Later, the girls would probably be returned to their individual rooms, to awaken next morning with festering green sores upon their flesh. Sores which they could not explain. Sores which suppurated green slime, exuded by the plant tendrils and deposited in the wounds!

That explained the girl who had died in Geoffrey's arms earlier that night. She must have regained consciousness while her flesh was being eaten by a plant. She had escaped, run away—only to die of fear and shock in Geoffrey's grasp.

The sheer malignity of the thing froze his marrow. Helplessly he watched the shrouded figure return to the elevator, evidently for a new cargo of unconscious human freight. The platform ascended in its shaft; the door slid shut. Now, except for the three unconscious girls, Geoffrey was alone.

A desperate plan came to him. Grimly he strove to force his gyved arms downward behind his back. His sinews, his muscles, ached agonizedly as he doubled over, contorted his body. Sweat poured into his eyes. But at last, success came to him. There was just enough chain between his handcuffs to enable him to draw his wrists past his feet. And now he had his fettered hands up in front of him.

Silently, desperately, he swayed to his feet. He reached down, grasped the heavy iron weight chained to his ankles. The long chain enabled him to lift it waist-high. Then he staggered with his burden, over to a spot beside the sliding door of the elevator-shaft.

He heard the whirring of machinery; saw the door beginning to slide open as the platform descended. He had just made his move in time!

He tensed himself, lifted the heavy iron weight to the full extent of his ankle chains. He waited—

The elevator door opened all the way. That black-shrouded figure stepped backward into the underground chamber, hauling the wheeled table on which three more unconscious, semi-nude girls lay. Geoffrey gripped his iron weight—and hurled himself straight at the unsuspecting back of the hooded, masked form.

"Now, Allister—!" he roared.

The weight bashed full into the spine of the black-shrouded figure. There came a crunching, sickening sound of pulped, smashed vertebrae; a weird ululation of death-agony ripped from a throat already in headlong descent to the fires of hell. The black-shrouded form collapsed, dead.

*LIKE* a flash, Geoffrey was on his knees beside his victim. He tugged the body over. His hand encountered something through the shroud—something rounded, soft, resilient, pliant—

A woman's breast!

The hooded, masked person was not a man! *It was a woman—a girl!*

Frenziedly, Geoffrey reached for the mask. Could this be Myrna Campbell? With his handcuffed hands he yanked away the hood and the mask.

And then—

"God in heaven!" Geoffrey Harde whispered. *"It's Alycia!"*

For one stricken instant he stared down into the dead, contorted, hate-twisted features of the woman he once had loved. Then, dazed and shaken, he found a key ring at her waist; found the key which unlocked his fetters. In a moment he had freed himself.

He raced to the three unconscious girls at the other side of the chamber, dragged them away from the green tendrils that drank their living blood. When he had pulled them from within reach of the carnivorous plants, he sped to the elevator. He pressed the control; the platform slowly ascended in its shaft.

It stopped at an upper floor inside the factory. Lying in the uncarpeted corridor, Geoffrey saw a dozen semi-nude, unconscious girls awaiting their turn to be taken into that hell-damned cellar. But there was one who was not unconscious. Her dark eyes were wide with fear. She was tied, hand and foot.

"Myrna—Myrna Campbell!" Harde whispered. He knelt beside her, unfastened her bonds, cradled her in his arms for a single moment. She welded her lips to his mouth, and her breasts were warm against his heaving chest…

Then he helped her to her feet. "Come! There's one more thing I must find out!" he whipped out.

*HE* led her out of the factory building and into his cousin's mansion. They raced upstairs. Geoffrey smashed into a certain bedroom, snapped on the light. He approached the bed on which Adam Allister lay—

"*Dead!*" Geoffrey gritted. "He's been dead for months! *He's embalmed!* That she-fiend, Alycia, kept him here to make people think he was still alive and merely ill—just as she fooled me! But Allister was dead all the time. He had nothing to do with *Parfum l'Enfer;* that must have been Alycia's creation. It was Alycia who discovered the strange flowers that drank human blood. It was Alycia who drugged her girl employees. And it was Alycia who wrote me that letter offering me a job! Adam Allister couldn't have written it, because he was dead!"

"But—but why did she want you to come here?" Myrna faltered.

"Because I was Adam's last surviving relative. With Allister dead, I might have tried to secure a share of the perfume business. Alycia didn't want me snooping around and perhaps discovering what she was up to. So she lured me here to kill me!"

Myrna crept into Geoffrey's arms. "And now—you'll inherit everything? You'll stop making *Parfum l'Enfer?* And you'll repay all those girls for what they've endured?"

Goeffrey smiled gently. "Yes. Everything will be done that can be done. There's only one thing more that must be settled." He looked into Myrna's dark, lustrous eyes; and his gaze held an unspoken query.

She smiled back at him and held up her lips for his kiss. And thus Geoffrey found his answer—and his happiness.

# ThIRST OF THE DAMNED

*One man loved her because she was beautiful.*
*The other sought her life as a slayer of babes, a*
*drinker of blood, as the Queen of the Witches!*

*H*E CREPT in like a shadow, noiseless, colorless. Murder was in his heart, mad, unreasoning murder, the lust to kill, to wring red blood from white flesh with cruel fingers. His shoulders were hunched, his neck drawn down. His nostrils quivered, his eyes glowed in the thick blackness of the still night.

Through the jimmied window he crept, trod softly on the carpeted floor of the bedroom. The ray of his flashlight found the face of the first sleeper. It swept from her clearly chiseled features down across the mounds of her breasts, the flatness of her stomach, like a great probing finger. The rumpled nightdress disclosed one tapering thigh, one rounded knee drawn up.

The light went off. Sinewy fingers of vengeance closed convulsively on the column of the sleeper's throat. The weight of his body crushed her thrashing limbs to the bed. Cruel fingers choked back her cries. Presently she struggled no longer.

Pit-pat, pit-pat on tiptoe through the dark room, into the hall, into another bedroom. The ray of the flash picked out the second sleeper. She might well have been the other's twin. The same thin, curved nose. The same high cheekbones, the same widely spaced eyes.

She stirred in her sleep. Boldly the intruder turned on the light. The sleeper opened her eyes. She must have read death in the menacing figure that hovered over her, must have known that her moments on earth were numbered. But she did not scream.

He tore the covers from about her shoulders. Long fingers twined in the black hair of her head to drag her from the bed.

Still she made no outcry. He ripped the thin nightdress half off her, gloated at her terror. Her breasts rose and fell, trembled and vibrated. With his clinched fists he hit her, again and again, until blood gushed from a shattered nose, trickled from her abused mouth.

Flung to the floor she lay still, only trembling breasts disclosing life. Swiftly he stooped, metal gleamed in his hand. Once—twice—thrice the knife rose and fell. Blood crimsoned white flesh, crimsoned the brown skin of the murderer's hand. Breathing stridently through his nose like a spent runner he cut and hacked....

A startled outcry in the doorway. Like an animal surprised at its kill the man turned. So! He hadn't killed the first one after all!

He leaped for her but she fled through the darkness, beat him to the front door and ran into the street screaming. Nearly a block he sped after her before the aroused townsmen pounced on him to bring him down, to save the girl from horror and death itself.

*A FLY* buzzed and droned against the smoke stained ceiling. The twelve men of the jury—twelve good men and true—each tried to look unconcerned. The baldheaded judge with the tobacco-stained goat's beard spat somewhere into the shadows behind his dais.

In answer to the clerk's shrill treble the prisoner arose. His face was pasty, yet stolid. All throughout the trial for murder that pasty face had been expressionless. The judge's droning voice sounded greatly like the fly that buzzed so aimlessly against the ceiling.

"—to hang by the neck until dead—dead—dead—and may God have mercy on your soul!"

For a tense moment there was silence in the courtroom. Each juryman breathed a little more stridently. Every reporter quit scribbling.

*"He! he! he!"* The shrill cackle of merriment swept across the courtroom. The principal witness for the prosecution, the woman whose tale had condemned the accused to the gallows, rocked with uncontrollable laughter.

The improvised press table was crowded by some thirty writers

*He crept toward her,
madness in his eye.*

from all parts of the nation who were covering this remarkable trial for millions of readers. Pencils poised at the sound of the laughter. There was no scratching, no sudden breathing. Only dead silence.

**EDDIE FLYNN** of the New York *Record* blanched at the sound of that laughter. He tried to keep his eyes fixed on the notes before him, but as a magnet attracts steel filings the laughing witness drew his unwilling gaze.

She sat just inside the rail, a tobacco-chewing bailiff on either side of her. Her red mouth was still parted in merriment but there was no laughter in her black eyes. They glowed with fire, with triumph, directly at Eddie Flynn. All during the trial those eyes had sought his. With an effort he broke away.

Now Boettner, the condemned man, was on his feet. His words were low but clear, directed not so much at the judge or the

courtroom but to the press table. For six days these men addressed had been sending thousands of words to millions of readers.

"You men and women," said the condemned murderer, "have laughed at us for a week. You have called us ignorant, superstitious backwoodsmen living three hundred years behind the times. Now I do not hear laughter among you." He paused, leaned forward intently. There was no move at the press table.

"In a few short weeks they will hang me by the neck until I am dead—dead—dead—. And you will say that my ignorance and superstition led me into this thing. All right, gentlemen, I will give you something to broadcast to your millions of readers. We Dutch do not talk much. We do not boast. But you may send out the word that the ignorant backwoodsman John Boettner who killed the hex woman because she was an evil, malignant thing is not the bumpkin you have painted him.

"You say I am an ignorant backwoodsman who believes in witches. Laugh at this, gentlemen. I am a graduate of two world-famous universities—*and I do believe in witches.* Is there no laughter now?

"Gentlemen, I am about to die. But tonight when you send your jeering dispatches remember this. The ignorant bumpkin is not sorry he killed. He slew no human being, no thing of flesh and blood. Rather he rid the world of a monster, an inhuman beast in the guise of a beautiful woman. I say it proudly, gentlemen, I killed her and I am glad. There is but one thing for which I am sorry."

Silence in the courtroom. The tobacco chewing judge had forgotten his gavel. The air was heavy with drama, pregnant with the words of the condemned murderer.

"Gentlemen—I did but half my job! If I had another opportunity I would cut the bleeding heart out of another, another who is worse than the first. With God as my witness, I tell you that woman standing there is as fiendish, as unnatural as her sister."

His skinny finger shot out dramatically to point at the black-eyed Hilda Vaard. White-faced she arose, as if pulled to her feet by some unseen force.

"Look at her," shrieked the condemned man. "I killed her sister because she bewitched me and mine. But I made a mistake by not killing them both! There is your drinker of blood, your slayer of babes, your witch in league with all the powers of hell! Damn her—"

His voice rose to a shriek. He clawed his way from the arms of the guards about him, was on the Vaard woman in the space of a split second. A claw-like hand tore the dress from her shoulder, the black material ripping like rotten cheesecloth to disclose white breasts that shrank from beneath the murderer's clawing fingers.

**EDDIE FLYNN** hurdled the table, beat the guards to the side of the madman. A right to the jaw. The maddened one crumpled to the floor. Flynn threw an arm protectively about Hilda Vaard. She breathed deeply there beside him for a moment. Her breasts rose and fell, drew Flynn's eyes.

His face turned white. His eyes bulged. There between the palpitant mounds of alabaster perfection was a splotch of brownish grey in the shape of a *bat*. A veined wing spread to either side to overlap the soft slope of a white breast. Even the bat's head, high in the dusky valley, was shaped perfectly. *And the thing was covered–with soft mouse-colored fur!*

Her hands were instantly crossed over the monstrosity. Black eyes held Flynn's. Was there an appeal for understanding in them or merely burning defiance?

All of this happened in split seconds. Before he knew what he did Flynn had his coat off and around the shoulders of the attacked woman shielding her nakedness. He shoved her roughly out of the craning courtroom without a word, across the street to the small drugstore and behind the prescription case.

"Iodine," he demanded from the pop-eyed clerk, and to the girl. "The fool scratched you. Mustn't take chances."

She let him take the coat from her shoulders. He tried not to shudder at the furred mark between her upthrust breasts, tried to swab the iodine on the scratches left by the nails of the condemned man. Her flesh was cold, held no glow. Finishing, he stood there lamely, fascinated by the white mounds.

"You missed a place," she said softly, and he saw. From the very mouth of the bat a tiny cut, deeper than the others, led downward. It bled, and the blood was deep purple rather than red. It looked as though the bat itself was bleeding at the mouth.

Before Flynn could move she placed her fingers over the bleeding cut, lifted them to her mouth. He saw the purple blood gleaming wet on her red lips, felt the electric shock of her hot gaze on his own staring eyes. Impulsively he leaned over and kissed her fingers. The blood on his own mouth was warm and salty.

"No!" he said and backed away. "No!"

Her greedy eyes were still on him. Not on his own eyes, not on his face, but peering intently at his throat. He dropped the cotton, the iodine, covered the base of his jugular vein with a trembling hand.

"No," he half shouted again and ran from the drugstore.

The evening heat was terrific. The descending sun was a hot furnace in a glowing copper bowl. Flynn paced his hotel room feeling feverish, worse than restless. For the twentieth time he went to the lavatory to rinse his mouth with antiseptic. He could not get Hilda Vaard out of his mind!

*IN* the back of his brain lingered the image of those twin mounds of white flesh with the furry mark disfiguring their smooth surface. His palms sweated remembering the cold softness of them, the smooth, furry feel of the mark. He threw himself on the couch, tried to blot out the memory of the girl by closing his hot eyes.

Tap—tap—tap at the door.

"Brother, you pick a fine time to sleep when the finest feature story of the year is breaking all around you!"

Flynn grunted and sat up. "You in again?"

Sheila Thames was small but not too small. She was rounded and curved where she should be, with a few extra soft turns thrown in for good measure. She sat down on the couch beside Flynn and rumpled his hair.

"Yeah, I'm in again, Eddie. Where have you been?"

"Right here trying to get some sleep."

"What did you do with the Queen of the Witches?"

Eddie snorted disdainfully. "A half-cracked story told by a madman, a murderer. That girl couldn't be hex. There isn't any such animal!"

Sheila lit a cigarette, eyed the recumbent man with grave eyes. She crossed her legs thoughtfully, revealing a long expanse of chiffon, topped by a gleaming few inches of white flesh.

"We're going to have company, Eddie. Young Henry Boettner, the killer's brother. Says he's going to show me something interesting."

Flynn sat up. "Nuts! I'm sick of the whole thing, I tell you! Fed up! Why ring me in on it?'

"Well, to be plain, I'm a little afraid of the light in Mr. Boettner's eye; so I'm having him sent to your room instead of mine."

A tap at the door interrupted. "That's the laddie now," she grinned and yelled, "Come in!"

Henry Boettner was younger than his brother. He sat stiffly across the room, dark eyes flashing back again and again at the white flesh shining above the girl's stocking top. Primly she pulled her skirt down.

*FIFTEEN* minutes later Flynn still lay listlessly in his room. The girl leaned over the documents on the table while Boettner's eyes stared in fascination at the shadowy valley revealed by her low-cut neck. The documents she peered at with so much interest were certificates of graduation from two world-famous universities inscribed with the name of John Boettner, the supposedly ignorant hex murderer.

"So you see, lady," went on the brother of the condemned man, "he was not the ignorant backwoodsman you paper people have made him! He is very close-mouthed, my brother, but I have decided to tell the things he would not. You do not believe in hex?"

The girl grinned. Flynn smiled and shrugged. Boettner went on gravely.

"For years we have lived as neighbors with the Vaards. When my brother first came back from abroad he was engaged to marry Martha Vaard, the eldest sister. What came between them I do not know, but the woman swore to avenge the jilting.

"After a few years, after the death of our own folks, Mrs. Vaard and the old man also died. John married an outsider. Her name was Janice. Martha Vaard came to the wedding, met the bride, won her confidence and became her friend.

"People around here will tell you that Janice, my sister-in-law, went mad. That is not so, lady. She was bewitched, hexed, little by little by her friend, Martha Vaard. You may laugh, but I tell now that it is God's truth! *Janice grew blood hungry.* First we missed chickens, then a dog, or a cat.

"Oh, John knew! He awakened once in the night to find his wife's teeth at his throat. He knew. He knew! She was hexed—bewitched by Martha Vaard! How do I know? Because Martha Vaard and her sister Hilda were the same way, the same things—drinkers of blood!"

Flynn threw back his head, laughed nervously. The Dutchman paused for a moment, resumed his gruesome story.

"My sister-in-law they sent to the asylum. But John has a boy by her. Peter, five years old. We could not keep him away from the Vaard's. Always they found a way to talk to him, to get him to wander to their home. We would lock the poor little fellow in his room and he would contrive a way to climb out. Like a monkey—or a ghost. He was hexed, I tell you, bewitched! No lock or key could hold him!

"Soon we became afraid. We found birds and little animals about our yard whose veins had been bitten into, whose blood had been drained. Little Peter we found on our front doorstep one night sleeping quietly with his mouth and hands covered with blood. What was there for my brother to do? *He killed the one responsible for this!*"

*A WAVE* of nausea swept over Flynn. Again into his mind flashed the vision of the Vaard girl as she had stood before him with her breasts bared, white and palpitant under his eyes. Again he felt the strange burning glow of her eyes as they centered on him. And again he saw the fur-covered mark, tasted the warm saltiness of her blood.

"Rot!" he almost shouted. "You're all a bunch of damned ignorant backwoodsmen. University degrees don't prove a thing to me. It was your brother that was mad, not Hilda Vaard."

The stolid Dutchman looked at him curiously. He spoke softly. "I think you have seen the Vaard woman too much, sir. You should be careful. She is *hex*."

"Get out, you fool!" Flynn leaped up, his face red. "It's fellows like you with your damned ignorant superstitions that keep an entire countryside upset for months. Without people like you there never would have been any killings. You, with your tales of hex and vampires and bloodsuckers! Get out, I say, get out! Damn it, I'm sick of it, fed up with the whole thing!"

After the murderer's brother left, he went to the lavatory to rinse his mouth again. Somehow the salty taste of blood persisted.

"So long, pal," said Sheila at the doorway. He thought she looked at him a little curiously.

*HE* ate his dinner alone, sullen and upset. Across the room he saw Sheila Thames eating with young Boettner, saw various others gather at the table to listen to Boettner's gruesome story, the inside dope on the newest hex murder.

Disgusted he left the room, sat in the lobby of the little hotel. Again he saw Boettner repeating the mad tale to any and all who would listen. He tried not to think of Hilda Vaard but even the meal he had eaten, the highballs he had consumed, would not wipe out the salty taste that still lingered in his mouth.

Despairingly he went to bed. The mental picture of twin mounds of white flesh danced and trembled before his eyes. Twin mounds that bore the imprint of a hairy bat on their sleek beauty, a hairy bat from whose mouth flowed purple blood.

The sound of running feet in the hallway awakened him. The moon was red, blood red, peering over the silent palms. The excited drone of low voices. Through the screened window he saw groups

*Her blood-red lips crept toward the pulsating jugular in his throat.*

of men clustered about the street lights below, groups that grew larger and larger with new arrivals.

He rang the bell for room service. No answer. He jiggled the phone hook disgustedly. No answer. Evidently the hotel force was too interested in whatever was transpiring to answer their guests. Muttering beneath his breath he put on his clothes and went down stairs.

As he went through the lobby Sheila Thames emerged from a telephone booth her face flushed, her eyes bright with excitement.

"What—?" he began.

"Listen," she said hurriedly, "get yourself an open line into New York right away. Things are going to happen here tonight! Little Peter Boettner has been murdered and the trail of blood leads to the hex woman's house! There'll be a lynching if they find her before the sheriff does!" She dashed out to the street before he could question her further.

For a moment longer he stood there, then hurried into the hastily reopened barroom for a drink. Henry Boettner, wild-eyed and gesticulating, was there. The sheriff was trying to calm him.

"Now calm down, Henry," he said. "We'll find her. She can't get away because we've got every road stopped up like a capped bottle. You keep on ranting and you'll have the folks so worked up they'll lynch her when we do find her. Take it easy!"

"Lynch her!" shouted the man. "Kill her! Tear her limb from limb! Poor little Peter! His throat! She tore it open with her pointed teeth, she drank his blood! Lynch her! Kill her!"

Flynn gulped his whiskey neat and left the room. Out on the street the talk was ominous. He knew it would be a sad fate that awaited Hilda Vaard if this gang of enraged citizens ever found her.

Sheila Thames laid a trembling hand on his sleeve.

"Come on," she said, "I want to show you something."

Back into the hotel, up the back stairway to Sheila's room. The room was dark but even in the blackness of the shadows Flynn grasped *her* presence. Sheila did not have to tell him that Hilda Vaard was in the room.

Swiftly Sheila drew down the cracked shades, lit the lamp. The girl Hilda stared at Flynn, not into his eyes, *but at the base of his throat where the pulse of his jugular throbbed and beat.*

Tap-tap-tap at the door. And again, louder, tap-tap-tap.

"Let me in, Miss Thames—it's Henry Boettner."

Without a word Sheila hustled Flynn and the woman into a narrow clothes closet, left the door open a tiny crack.

*FLYNN,* afterward, was never aware of what went on in the room. He was conscious only of the woman pressed so closely to him in the cramped, stifling closet. The smell of her, the feel of her, the sense of her. Her breath on his cheek was cold. She shivered a little beside him there, one rounded thigh touching his, her soft body burning against him.

When his arm went about her protectively, her hand came up through the darkness of the closet to caress his cheek, to touch his half open mouth with gentle fingers, to slide down his chin to the base of his throat where his pulse played.

And to his own self-horror, when Sheila had gotten rid of her visitor and flung open the closet door, he found himself caressing the Vaard woman, his fingers sliding gently over the contours of her flaming cheeks down to the base of her soft throat.

Sheila Thames was tense with excitement. "You can't stay here," she half moaned. "Eddie, you'll have to get her out and away somewhere. That man suspects something! You'll have to take my car and get her away!"

"I know a place they'll never find me," said Hilda. Her voice was dreamy, her eyes blazing with fire, *centered on Flynn's throat.*

*THE* flight through the back alleys of the sweltering little town to the spot where the newspaper woman's car awaited was hazy in Flynn's mind. Like an episode occurring to someone else. Only dimly he recalled the roadster roaring out of an alley to nearly run down a group of idling men who talked in the blue light of an overhead arc. One of the group recognized the white-faced woman who crouched in the seat beside Flynn.

They were hardly on the highway before the lights of the pursuing cars lit the road behind them.

*"They'll never find me where we're going," she told him.*

At the woman's suggestion Flynn switched off the lights a little farther along. Again at her bidding he wheeled the roadster into a weed-grown side road, sat there silently while pursuit swept by.

"Now where?" He was all too conscious of her nearness.

"Straight ahead, on down this road."

It was hardly a road. But straight down the dim wheel tracks Flynn headed the car. His sense of smell soon told him where they were going. He turned inquiring eyes on his silent companion. She nodded.

"They'll never catch us in the swamp. I know it like the palm of my hand!"

Even then it didn't occur to the man to wonder *how* she knew it. Or even to wonder if she had really committed the crime for which the mob was pursuing her.

*AN* hour later the only human sound was the noise made by the pole as he pushed the light *pirogue* through the stagnant waters of the swamp. The channel of the stream was almost indistinguishable for the draping Spanish moss made the passageway a roofed tunnel. Between interlaced branches a red moon peeped knowingly. Mangrove bushes and palmetto fronds were thick among the higher places.

The eerie cry of a swamp bird. Snake-like vines hanging from towering cypress trees. Crouched in the prow of the *pirogue* the woman's face was ghastly white. Only her eyes were alive.

"Here," she said softly, and Flynn pushed the blunt nose of the craft upon a hummock. The black ooze of the swamp sucked at his feet as he clambered ashore after her. She grasped his hand with deathly cold fingers. He followed blindly.

Thorns that were daggers in miniature cut and tore at them. With a ripping sound her silk skirt split thigh high. A tapering leg emerged to gleam pale and white in the ghastly light. Another thorn tore through the sleeve of her dress leaving a bleeding wound in its wake. Flynn saw—and licked his lips nervously.

Presently the terrain grew firmer, the mud less viscous. The cypresses and the shrubbery that clutched at their passing bodies thinned. Straight ahead on a large hummock he saw the sloping roof of a swamp cabin, black, moss-covered. She stopped, breathed deeply, almost a sigh.

"They will never look for us there," she said. "That place belongs to the Boettners themselves!"

She led the way again.

Almost to the shack she stumbled, sprawled full length in the mud and ooze. With a little startled exclamation of pain or fright she rolled quickly aside. Too late. The swamp moccasin that had sunk its poisonous fangs into the soft flesh of her breast glided away with the speed of disappearing light.

Flynn gathered her in his arms, carried her to the shack.

It cost interminable time to fumble for and find the kerosene lamp. She sat white-faced, horrified, in a chair by the rickety table. He tore the thin dress from her, used its few remaining dry portions to swab the mud and slime from her upper torso.

At the mouth of the furry bat two tiny pin pricks of blood gleamed red in the lamplight.

"What'll we do?" he asked frantically.

"You have a knife?"

He nodded, read the answer to his futile question in her half-glazed eyes.

With trembling fingers he opened the little wounds, thrust the steel blade deeply into the soft flesh, until blood trickled forth in two steady streams. She neither winced nor moved but watched him with glowing eyes. He bent to suck the deadly poison from her veins. Blood, thick and redolent in his nostrils, salty-sweet in his mouth, warm and heavy on his tongue.

*It was as if he kissed the bloody mouth of the furred bat.*

Her hands were in his hair, drawing his head closer and closer to her flesh. Her eyes were glazed; his, half closed. The scent of her, the taste of her, the feel of her. Soft fingers searched along the base of his throat, rested on the pulsing blood vein. She sighed.

*THE* door flew open. Outlined there was Henry Boettner. Behind him the horror-stricken eyes of Sheila Thames.

"Now, damn you," yelled Boettner, "I've got you!" He threw up the heavy revolver to fire but the woman behind him seized his arm. The gun roared but the bullet tore its way into the floor. Boettner screamed again with rage, slapped the newspaper woman against the wall. His eyes were mad, demented as he turned, sneering to the other two.

"So she's got *you*, too, Flynn! You're another one of the damned bloodsuckers! I'm going to kill you both, damn you, both of you."

The gun came up again.

Flynn crouched on his haunches and waited for the bullet to crash into his flesh. He did not even look at Boettner. He was gazing at Sheila Thames who was slowly struggling to her feet.

A tiny trickle of red, red blood wormed its way down from the corner of her mouth. He saw the blue veins of her upper breast where the waist had torn on a nail in the wall. He saw her pulsing jugular vein and licked his lips.

He wanted to live—*wanted to live so he could taste the blood of Sheila Thames.*

Hilda Vaard, the hex woman, walked slowly toward Boettner. The lower part of her body was still covered with the slime and ooze of the swamp. Her eyes were black points that burned, boring and drilling into those of the man with the gun.

"I'm going to shoot—" he warned her.

Step by step she moved towards him. Her breasts quivered and swayed, shook and vibrated with every motion of her body. The man's fascinated eyes were riveted upon the furry mark on her chest.

Boettner screamed hoarsely, dropped the gun, turned and ran into the night.

Flynn crept toward Sheila Thames, madness in his eyes. He grabbed her as she started out the door. Superhuman strength was in his hands as he flung her across the table, crashing the light to the floor. Madly he tore at the clothes on her white body, convulsively sinking his fingers into soft flesh. His lips on her throat, his teeth—

A blinding flash of pain, a great light before his eyes, and blackness.

*A FEW* days later Eddie Flynn had visitors. He sat propped up in a hospital bed, wan and burned out by a raging fever.

"Well," said Sheila sympathetically, "you'll probably be interested in knowing that Henry Boettner confessed. He killed his own nephew to put the blame on Hilda Vaard. He's hated her ever since she refused to have anything to do with him years ago. He did all the blood acts that were committed in Leonville simply to ruin the Vaards. They're going to lock him up in an asylum."

Flynn shuddered and drew his pajama coat closer together across his chest.

The girl continued. "That's the trouble with all these damn mystery stories. They always turn out to be explainable, nothing supernatural about them. Say, fellow, what are you looking at?"

Flynn tore his tortured eyes away from the low-necked dress, eyes that gloated over the tiny pulse throbbing at the base of a white throat.

"*Hex,*" she sneered, "is a lot of baloney!"

He nodded miserably, tugged the coat even higher. He wanted to hide from the eyes of all the little furry mark on his chest that was constantly growing larger. *Already he thought it resembled vaguely a spread-winged bat!*

JUSTIN CASE

# DOOM DOOR

*She was a hot number in a waterfront beer
joint. And he was a very tough ladies' man—
until he killed one woman to love another*

*HE MET* the girl in a beer joint where she was hustling foam-topped glasses to shirtless longshoremen who leaned over dirty tables and leered at her. When she came to the booth to take his order, he grinned drunkenly and hung onto her bare arm. "Listen babe," he drooled. "What time do you get through here?"

She stared at him. She could have wrenched her arm loose, shrilled a command to one of the bar-tenders and had him thrown out of the place. But she stared at him. Joe Venullo wasn't bad to look at.

Neither was she. She was a short, slim thing with hard young breasts that were apparent under the dirty white of her shirtwaist. Her skirt was tantalizingly short, almost revealing the rolled tops of her cheap stockings; firm, rounded thighs undulated when she walked. Joe Venullo had seen prettier faces, but this one with its tight red lips and dark eyes possessed something more than prettiness.

"What's it to you?" the girl said.

"Well," Joe grinned, "I got an evening to waste in this lousy town, and I figured maybe we could get to know each other."

That started it. They spent the evening at a cheap dance hall in the slums, went from there, at midnight, to a sordid little slum hotel where Joe Venullo wrote in the register: Mr. and Mrs. Joseph Fenno. The girl laughed at that when they were alone in their room.

Her name was Valma. "Down around the joint where I work,

they call me Billy," she said. "Gee, Joe!…" She smiled. The light in her eyes inflamed him.

They killed a pint of gin together, and Billy took the last drink standing before the dressing table mirror, holding the glass to her mouth with one hand while she patted her flat, firm stomach appreciatively with the other. "Like me?" she said, smiling.

Joe liked her. She was, he told himself, different from most of the girls he had picked up on his frequent trips to the city. She had come with him willingly, without a lot of dumb arguments, and she was willing now to be sociable.

*"I guess he had it coming to him," Billy said.*

He walked drunkenly toward her and took her in his arms. "You're swell," he said. "Kill that drink and then—"

She didn't object when he grabbed her, or when he helped himself to a long, intimate kiss, sliding his hand down her back toward her hips. She said: "I think you're swell, too, Joe."

**THEY** left the hotel at four in the morning, and made a date to see each other a week later.

It went on for a month. Then she said: "Do you realize, Joe honey, I don't know a thing about you?"—and Joe stiffened. He hadn't told her much; had been careful not to. He hadn't told her, for instance, that he was married to Agnes and lived in a small house back off the State road, some twelve miles outside the city.

He hadn't told her that he, Joe Venullo, had lived there for

three years on money which had been stolen from a man who had lain dead, for that same length of time, under six feet of murder-earth—or that the police were still looking for the murderer.

No, he hadn't mentioned those things. But he had thought about them plenty, and had thought along other lines as well. "Listen, babe," he said now. "How about you and me getting married?"

She was in his arms when he said that, in the back seat of a hired sedan on a lonely road near the waterfront. She said: "Joe! Honest?" and then looked into his eyes and crushed her hot mouth against his and kept it there Joe's hands went to her waist and crept higher, gripping her fiercely.

"Sure thing, babe," he told her. "We'll talk it over next week."

*IT* was daylight when he got home, and Agnes said queerly: "Again you've been out all night, Joe?"

That was all she ever said: "Again you've been out all night, Joe?" More than once he had wondered if she suspected the truth. She stood now in front of the big electric refrigerator in the kitchen and poured milk into a glass and handed it to him. "You look tired out," she said.

The dog—the German police dog which Joe Venullo hated with all his heart—stretched out from under the stove and growled low in its throat, eyeing Joe with a hatred equal to his own.

Joe looked at his wife. She wore a dirty kimono and she was fat underneath it. She had let herself get fat like that since he had married her two years ago and brought her to this house to live. Fat and slovenly, and more so every day. Yet she was no older than he. No older than Billy.

Her breasts wobbled under the kimono when she walked, and they were heavy, low breasts that were no longer smooth and white, no longer fascinating. Her hips had grown large, too; her thighs had lost their form—were thick, bulky.

"Tonight," Joe thought, "I'll do what I've been thinking of for the past two weeks."

After supper he went downstairs to the cellar and cleaned refuse out of the coal bin. The coal bin had a dirt floor. He tested the floor with a shovel and found it soft, and nodded his head approvingly. When Agnes called down to him and said: "Joe, what are you doing?" he did not answer.

Later he said: "You better go to bed and not wait for me. I don't feel like goin' upstairs yet."

"But Joe, you were away all last night and I was so lonesome. I'm your wife, Joe."

"I'll be up later," Joe said. "You go to sleep. I'll wake you up."

She went upstairs alone, and when he walked into the bedroom an hour later she was awake and waiting for him. "Joe!" she whispered. "My own Joe!" She wore nothing but a thin robe, and her fleshy body rolled heavily as she turned to stretch her arms toward him.

"Okay," Joe said. "Sure. I'm here."

As he stood near her his muscles grew tense and nervous. Doing this thing he had planned to do was not going to be so easy, he thought. For one thing, Agnes was strong enough to put up a good fight and she had lungs that could do a lot of loud screaming.

"I missed you last night, babe," he lied.

"Joe! Did you?"

"Sure I did." He sat down on the bed next to her, put his arm under her body and squeezed. She laughed and gasped for breath when he did that, but she enjoyed it. Her arms went around his neck and pulled him down, crushing his face against hers.

"It's a long time since you acted as if you loved me, Joe."

"Tonight I'll make up for it," he told her—reluctantly, because he was eager to get that other thing over with. Then he thought: Hell, I might just as well be good to her; it's the last time. He patted her shoulder and let his hands go around her to cross caressingly behind her shoulder blades…. She began breathing noisily, and her hungry kisses were suckingly audible.

*LATER*, when he stretched himself and stood erect, his wife was asleep. He stared down at her and grinned and then looked at his hands, working them to put strength into them. Bending over his wife's body, he slid his hands over her fleshy shoulders and curled his fingers around her neck; squeezing hard with his thumbs.

She awoke, screaming, but he grinned down into her contorted face and squeezed all the harder. When she writhed on the bed, he put a knee in the middle of her stomach and shifted his whole weight onto the knee until the bed groaned.

His fingers kept closing tighter; his thumbs sank deeper into the thick flesh of his wife's throat, until her screams became wet choking sounds that had hard work getting past the swollen purple blockade of her tongue.

When she stopped squirming, he leaned heavily on her and locked his finger-like steel claws to make sure that the job was

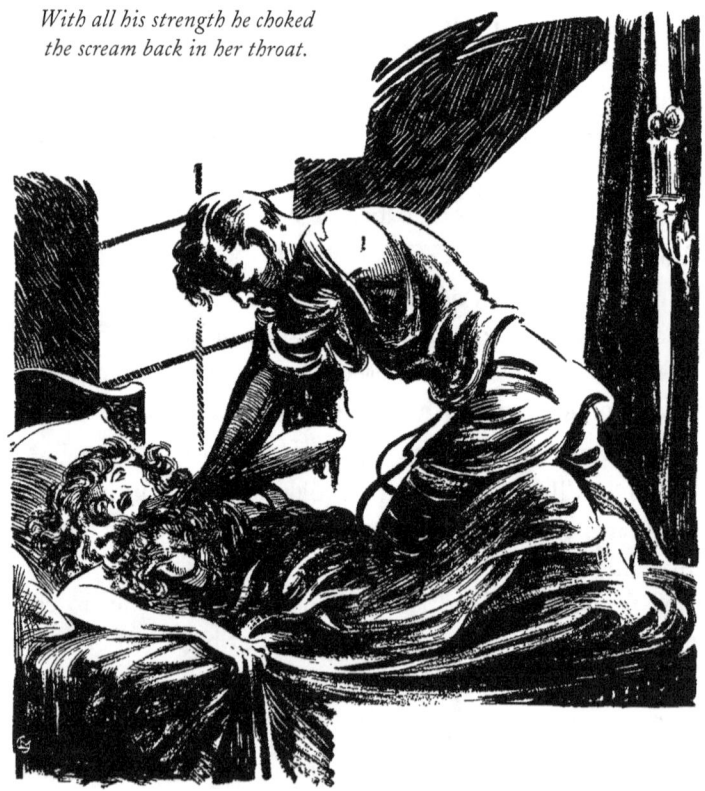

*With all his strength he choked the scream back in her throat.*

thoroughly finished. Then, grinning, he kissed the livid thumb-marks on her neck.

He carried the corpse of his murdered wife downstairs to the cellar. It was heavy. When he got it to the foot of the stairs he dumped it to the floor and dragged it the rest of the way to the coal bin.

While he was digging a deep hole for it, the German police dog came silently downstairs and sniffed at the corpse and then lay in the middle of the cellar floor, watching him.

"You get to hell out of here!" Joe snarled, but the dog did not move.

Joe finished his task and then raked the cellar floor and shoveled refuse back into the bin. Then he went upstairs, he heated water on the oil stove in the kitchen, washed his hands and face and cleaned the damp earth off his shoes. From the refrigerator he took a pint bottle half full of gin and emptied it. The dog lay under the stove and watched him.

"I'll tend to you right now," Joe said.

He tied a rope to the dog's collar and led the animal outside, through the woods and across a long, sloping field that lay pale in the moonlight. He took the dog a mile from the house to a little bridge that spanned a deep stream. He secured a heavy boulder and twisted and knotted the rope around it. The dog seemed to divine his purpose and began to growl ominously. Hair began to bristle on the back of his neck.

Joe picked up the boulder and heaved it over the four by four which served as a guard at the edge of the bridge. The dog was jerked off his feet and whisked out of sight. There was only one sharp yelp then a heavy splash.

When Joe got home he locked the door and went upstairs to the room where he had murdered his wife. "Well, that's that," he said. Then he sprawled out on his wife's death bed and went to sleep.

*A WEEK* later Joe Venullo said: "Listen, babe. I was out lookin' for a house. I got a swell place about twelve miles outside the city, just back off the State road. You'll love it."

When he said that, he was in the beer joint where Billy worked, and Billy was leaning over the table to slide a glass of beer under his grinning face. Billy drew a deep, noisy breath into her slender body and said: "Joe! Honest?" and her hard little breasts swelled to flesh-firm cones under the dirty front of her dress.

Joe curled an arm around her waist and pushed a fist gently into her stomach. "Sure thing, babe," he said. "You can throw up your job tonight and we'll get hitched tomorrow."

The next afternoon he took Billy to a J.P. and slipped a ten-cent-store ring over her third finger. Married, they went into the house where another woman lay dead under the cellar floor, and he said to her: "There you are, honey. All ours and all furnished. The guy and his wife that used to live here moved out last week and I got the joint for a song. Like it?"

"Gee, it's swell!"

"You're pretty swell yourself," Joe said, and kissed her.

While he was kissing her, with her small body trembling against his own and her dark eyes wide open with yearning, he thought queerly: It's a damn' good thing she don't know what's down cellar… yeah, it's a damn' good thing she don't!

They went upstairs together and Billy said: "Who's this, Joe?"

She was pointing to a photograph on the dressing table. The photograph was of Agnes. In straightening the house out, Joe had forgotten to remove it. He caught a quick breath now, relaxed before Billy noticed it, and said easily: "Sister of mine. Why? Want me to heave it out?"

"Why no, Joe. Of course not." Billy held the picture in her small hands and scrutinized it closely. "She's nice looking, isn't she?"

"Yeah, kind of. But she ain't in your class, babe."

"You think I'm good-lookin', Joe?"

He said: "You're darn right I do!" and pulled her toward the bed where the girl in the photograph had been strangled by his own strong hands. The hands did other things—more pleasant things—now. They pressed Billy against him; they squeezed her and caressed her, rough and gentle by turns. Billy snuggled closer.

"You and me are goin' to get along swell, kid," Joe told her.

He went to sleep with his head pillowed in the soft hollow of her shoulder above her breast, thrilling to the warm, throbbing satin of her skin. Her arms were tight around him, holding him there.

*BUT* that night, darkness made a difference.

Perhaps it was more than the darkness. Perhaps it was partly due to the photograph on the dressing table. Joe stared at the photograph—stared more at it than he did at Billy—and that was strange. Other times he had been savagely thrilled with expectation, watching Billy's every movement while she slid out of her dress, tugged the cheap stockings from her slender legs, unfastened the snaps of the brassiere which encased her lilting breasts.

Tonight he was nervous. His fingers were wobbly and sudden tremors like chills shook him. He stared at the photograph, forced himself to focus the gaze of his twitching eyes on Billy, and then, in spite of himself, kept looking uneasily at the picture again.

Even the thrill of having Billy in his arms, crushed hard against him with all the fervor of her amorous enthusiasm, failed to rid his mind of the unpleasant thoughts that wormed there. Even Billy's hungering mouth against his own… the questing warmth of her lips on his…

Because he was nervously alert, he heard the sound from downstairs when under ordinary circumstances it might have gone unnoticed. A door had clicked open down there.

Joe stiffened, sat up in bed, and supported the weight of his body on rigid arms. A door had opened downstairs! But he had locked both the front and the back, and the house had no other entrances.

"What is it, Joe?" Billy whispered. "What's the matter?"

"Shut up. Listen."

He was listening for footsteps. If a door had opened—and a door *had* opened!—it meant that someone had opened it. Once before, when the woman beside him had been Agnes, not Billy, a tramp had entered the house late at night through the front door which Agnes had left unlocked. He, Joe Venullo, had crept downstairs and caught the tramp in the act of raiding the electric refrigerator.

But tonight he himself had locked both doors. He knew they were locked. And yet—a door had clicked open.

He waited, and heard no sound. Beside him Billy was breathing heavily, her face hot and damp against his shoulder. "What is it, Joe?" she whispered again, fearfully.

He did not answer. He started to but the reply froze in his throat because, downstairs, the door had clicked shut again. He pushed Billy away from him, swung erect. In a dozen silent strides he was across the bedroom, over the threshold and pawing the bannister at the head of the stairs.

It was dark down there. Tonight the darkness seemed alive, seemed sinister. But what the hell!—that was just his own imagination, because he'd been thinking too long about the thing in the cellar. If a tramp had broken into the house, he, Joe Venullo, was big enough to toss the guy out again, easy.

Still, he went down the stairs slowly, on the balls of his bare feet, and his eyes were big in his head, staring. Maybe the thing down there wasn't a tramp. Maybe it had come up from the cellar....

He went nervously into the kitchen and pulled the light chain, peered around him. He opened the closet door and made sure that no one was hiding there. Then he went and tried the front door and the back door. Both doors were locked. Both keys were in their slots, on the inside.

"Guess I was hearin' things," he muttered.

He went to the cellar door and opened it, and thumbed the switch that turned on the light down there He didn't go down. His hands and arms were shaking more violently now than when he had first slid out of bed. Cold sweat had oozed from his pores, chilling him.

He didn't go down. He was afraid to. He went back upstairs.

"You're cold, Joe," Billy said, cuddling against him.

"Yeah, it's chilly down there," he mumbled.

That was the beginning.

*THE* next night he stared again at the photograph on the dressing table and said: "Listen, babe. I guess maybe I'll chuck that thing out."

"But why, Joe? I don't mind havin' it there as long as she's your sister. I think it's kind of nice."

He left it there and kept still about it. He was afraid she would get curious and ask too many questions.

He didn't sleep. Knowing that he needed sleep, he vented his restlessness on the girl beside him; and he was so rough with her, so hungry with his lips, so savage with his embrace, that he frightened her into saying: "Joe, what's wrong with you? You're hurting me!"

Hurting her? He laughed at that, and thought of what his hands had done to the woman who lay downstairs. "You got to learn to take it, babe," he said. "I guess I'm built that way." But he knew, even without turning the light on to look, that his lips had left crimson imprints on her throat, and his clutching fingers had bruised her tender flesh.

Then, downstairs, the door opened.

Joe lay rigid. Breath stuck in his throat and went cold there, and the heart under his ribs began to sledge with the force of a pile driver. A door had opened! And this time he was sure of it. He had heard the dull, metallic click of the latch and knew that the sound was not spawned in his imagination.

But tonight, before coming upstairs to bed, he had made certain that both doors and every window in the house were locked!

He lay motionless, stiff as wood except for the trip hammer pounding of his heart, and listened. Billy said in a frightened voice: "Joe, what's eatin' you?"

Downstairs, the door thudded shut again.

This time Billy heard it, too. "Joe!" she whispered. "Someone's downstairs!" But Joe was out of bed, grimly pulling open the top drawer of the dressing table where the photograph of his dead wife sat and smiled at him. He took out a palm-fitting automatic and went downstairs.

The doors and windows were locked. The house was empty.

With cold salt sweat beading his forehead and trickling into his staring eyes, Joe went slowly down the cellar stairs and paced toward the coal bin. For a long while he stood in the narrow entrance and looked down at the floor, while the glow from a dangling lamp bulb spilled over his shoulder and illuminated the pile of refuse that lay there.

"I'm goin' nuts," Joe mumbled. "Nuts...."

The bin was just as he had left it after shoveling refuse back over the hard packed earth which covered the corpse.

He tested the cellar windows and found them locked. In one of them a pane of glass was missing; he himself had broken it, months ago, and pulled out the jagged edges. But the aperture, was small, far too small for any intruder to wriggle through. Besides, the sound that Joe Venullo had twice heard while lying in bed—the sound that was slowly shaking him loose from his mind—had been the dull double click of a door opening and then closing. A door.

But the front door and the back door were both locked. Locked with the keys on the inside. How, in the name of God...?

He went back to Billy and she said fearfully: "What was it, Joe? What was it that opened the door?"

"I don't know," Joe mumbled. But he was staring at the photograph on the dressing table, and even in the dark the eyes of the woman in the picture seemed to be leering at him as if they, and they only, knew the answer.

*ALL* the rest of the night Joe lay awake, bathed in cold sweat. The next day his eyes were deep-sunk with exhaustion.

When Billy came to him that morning and said, "I think I'll straighten things out around here," Joe did not offer to help her. He sat in the kitchen and stared at the door leading to the cellar.

"She's dead," he kept telling himself. "She couldn't be no deader. It ain't possible for her to come hack!" But he was not sure.

That evening he said to Billy: "Listen, babe, let's you and me go some place and get tight. This place is gettin' on my nerves."

Billy glanced at him queerly. "Sure, Joe. Sure," she said.

*"It's her!" he screamed.
"She's come back!"*

At two-thirty in the morning when they got home, Joe was drunk, but drunk as he was he made sure that the front door, the back door, and all the windows were securely fastened. Then he went reeling upstairs; and for the first time since he had known her, Billy was reluctant to come to him. Only partly undressed, she stood there, trembling a little and staring at him.

"You're—awful drunk, Joe," she whispered.

"Bein' drunk is good for a guy's nerves," he told her. "It keeps him from goin' nuts."

"But Joe—"

He wasn't listening; he jerked Billy hard against him, his hands mauling over the pulsing hot sleekness of her tempting curves.

At first she resisted; then her hard little body began, as it always did, to tremble.

"I do love you, Joe," she whispered. "Honest."

He kneaded his mouth against hers and his fingers made livid red blotches on the small of her back. He was drunk, and knew it, and there was nothing gentle in the savage clutch of his fingers. But when Billy would have protested, the words went from her pain-twisted mouth into his and were stifled there. And the liquor within him induced perspiration that seeped through the pores of his body and made him hotter, drunker.

And then, downstairs, the door opened.

The room was dark; Billy had reached out and put a hand on the light switch before crowding over against the man she loved. The room's only light was moonlight, filtering through the window beside the dressing table and slanting palely across the bed, across the floor beyond, to climb faintly up the wall near the door.

Joe Venullo heard the dull, significant click from downstairs and pushed himself up on stiff arms and stared at the door. Stark terror chilled the sweat that gleamed on his tense body.

"It's her," he mumbled. "It's her again. It couldn't be no one else. I locked the doors...."

*MOONLIGHT* painted a pale pattern on the wall beside the door. In its yellow shadows a face took form—a face that might perhaps have swayed there above a body that stood invisible in the gloom of the doorway.

It was an indistinct face, floating there in shadows, unreal and yet horribly like another face which only a few nights ago had swelled into a writhing, wretched mask of agony under Joe Venullo's strangling fingers.

He stared at it. His rigid arms held him up and his cold body was hooked at the stomach; his legs were rotten—weak, yet stiff as wood. He stared at the face and knew what it was.

His eyes grew to enormous size in their fleshy sockets. His mouth jerked open, drooling saliva that trickled down a tongue which tried frantically to scream out the terror in Joe Venullo's heart. His arms began to tremble, then shook violently, jarring his chest and head so that his hair, the whole mop of it, wriggled into his eyes and hung there.

"It's her!" he shrieked. "My God, it's her!"

The face there in the shadows of the doorway—the face that hung distorted and unreal in the pale shaft of moonlight from the window—was the face of the woman he had murdered.

Joe Venullo hurled himself to his feet, dragging the bedclothes with him. "She come up from the cellar!" he screamed. "She's been comin' up every night! The door's been open…." The bedclothes tangled around him as he lurched up from his knees and staggered against the wall, staring. He shook them loose, took a stumbling step backward. "Leave me alone!" he croaked. "Don't come no closer!"

*WALKING* almost on his knees, his chest heaving and his terror-filled eyes glowing like wet hard agates, he got to the dressing table where, in the top drawer, he kept the palm-fitting automatic which had once—or perhaps more than once—made murder. But then he was no longer alone. Billy was groping through the shadows toward him, her arms outstretched, her lips mumbling his name.

She, too, was afraid, but her fear was for Joe Venullo. Her small, hard body was trembling as she flung herself against Joe and clung to him in terror.

"What's the matter with you?" she asked him. "For God's sake, what's got into you?"

He hit her in the pit of the stomach and sent her crashing against the end of the bed. But even that did not silence her.

"Joe!" Somehow she got in his way. Somehow her love for him was bigger than the terror that shrilled, unchecked, in her wailing enunciation of his name. She flew at him, got her hands on him, and tried to stop him in his mad rush for the door.

But Joe Venullo was mad. Gaping at the face that floated there before him in the yellow murk near the door, he saw in Billy only a scheming accomplice of the thing which had come up out of the cellar to destroy him.

"You devil!" Joe shrieked. "Leave go of me!" Then his hands

swept out and his unclean fingernails sank deep into Billy's smooth, warm flesh. He swiped at her with the gun in his other fist, and missed. He kicked her, hurled her aside with such force that her bleeding body made thunder against the dressing table, knocking to the floor the photograph which had stood there.

The face in the shadows was gone then, but Joe did not realize it. He hurled himself at the door, intent only on getting out of the room where the thing from the cellar had come to destroy him. Twice, blindly, he fired at the place where the face had floated.

The bullets shattered flawed glass in a cheap mirror which hung there on the wall. The glass crunched under Joe's feet as he blundered over the threshold. Pawing the wall, he lurched to the head of the stairs, flung himself down them. But it was dark there, and there was no pale glow of moonlight to lessen the darkness... and the stairs were steep.

Joe Venullo stumbled on the top step. The gun exploded, then spun from his hand, and clattered down the staircase ahead of him. The prolonged shriek of agony that welled from Joe's throat was smothered by the thunder of his hurtling body.

He crashed downward, tore railing posts loose and broke plaster from the wall. He screamed until his twisted body struck the floor at the base of the stairs. Then his screams became bloody gurgles and the crimson froth in his throat strangled him. He crawled, battered and broken and dying, into the kitchen, and collapsed.

*HE* was dead when two uniformed officers in a State Police car came to the house an hour later, after picking up, on the State Highway, a near-naked, sobbing girl who said her name was Billy. Joe Venullo was dead. His body was broken and twisted from its plunge down the stairs. Blood had congealed around a jagged bullet hole in his chest.

"He—he shot himself when he tripped on the stairs," Billy said. "I heard the gun go off...." Then she said; "He went crazy. Honest to God, he just went nuts all of a sudden. A door opened downstairs, like it's been doin' every' night since we been here, and then I seen Joe lookin' in the mirror, and then he went out of his mind. I guess I was partly to blame, because when I was movin' things around this afternoon I hung the mirror there and

I moved the picture on the dressin' table… and he seen the picture in the mirror and thought it was someone comin' for him.…

The two State Troopers went upstairs to investigate. When they returned to the kitchen, the girl named Billy was standing very still and stiff near Joe Venullo's body, staring at the cellar door. The door was open. Someone, or something, was climbing the dark stairs.

One of the troopers drew a gun and took a stiff step forward. He stopped, spat out a breath of relief, and relaxed. Out of the cellar's gloom came a dog, a German police dog, who gazed dispassionately around him, then padded quietly across the floor and sniffed at Joe Venullo. A ten-foot length of rope with a mess of frayed and knotted loops, trailed behind the dog.

The dog growled ominously. Having hated Joe in life, he still hated him.

He turned, walked to the refrigerator and put his front feet, both of them, on the door-release pedal that extended, at floor level, from the cabinet. The door opened with a dull click that could be heard easily, in the stillness of the night, as far as the bedroom upstairs.

The dog sniffed, found meat on the second shelf and dragged it out. He closed the door by rearing on his hind legs and pushing the weight of his body against it.

"Well, I'll be damned!" one of the troopers said.

*THE* dog turned, went down the cellar stairs with the meat clamped in his jaws. Both troopers followed him. The dog went quietly across the cellar floor, took a running start, gained a window-ledge and vanished like a gaunt gray ghost through an aperture where one pane was missing.

"Well, I'll be damned!" one of the troopers said again.

He paced forward, stood at the edge of a shallow hole where the dog had pushed aside a pile of refuse and pawed the damp earth. Something white gleamed there. Something white and swollen that looked like a human arm. The trooper reached down, stiffened, and jerked his hand away. Then, scowling, he reached down again, seized the white thing and pulled on it.

The girl named Billy, who had come timidly down the cellar stairs, stared with widening, white-rimmed eyes and put both hands hard against the throbbing, blood-smeared mounds of her breasts. In a hoarse whisper she said: "My—God! I guess Joe had it comin' to him…."

E. HOFFMANN PRICE

# DAWN OF DISCORD

*He went back into time to find the beginnings
of hatred and war—to cut it short and end the
horrors of modern times... only to find that love
and hate and death were queerly distorted.*

*TIME WAS* a dimension of space: time was a closed curve, without beginning or end, and space was curved, endless, yet finite. Or so John King had told himself, during those years of study. But now, with war threatening to overwhelm the world, King was through with theory. He was going back into time—or space—or both, if his equations did not lie, and he was going to stop war at its origin.

He took off his acid-stained smock and put on a khaki shirt, breeches, laced boots. King was incongruous among the switchboards and oscillation tubes, the retorts and electric furnaces of the laboratory in the old house on top of Russian Hill; he looked like a man ready to invade the jungle, and he was tall and lean and fit enough for such a task.

One look at the broad bay, at the housetops far below him, at the bridges that spanned the water; one pang of regret as he paused at the door of adventure. His fanatic devotion to science had kept him a stranger to women, and though he resolutely kept them from his thoughts, he wished that he could be sure of returning. There was a shapely blonde girl who must work in an office nearby; he had tried not to notice her on his way to the restaurant where he ate during the afternoon breathing spell.

Then he turned toward the time-traveling machine which was to take back an age when there was no such thing as war. Arrived there, King would cut war off at its root.

The machine had thick metal walls and was shaped like a bathysphere; its glass ports were built to resist enormous pressure, and it was powered by atomic energy. This would be nothing like the flight of an airplane or rocket ship; there would be no travel in the ordinary sense of the word, for King was putting himself into a magnetic field which would reverse time. This would not be like any three dimensional journey that any man had ever made.

The self-locking door closed behind him. King wanted to look back once more at the present, but he feared that he would falter; so be stepped to the control levers and the dials that filled all the bulkheads. Two people could have found room beside him, provided they were slender.

He closed the switch; a surge of power shook the machine, and the daylight that came in through the ports became green, then a gray blur. Every atom of his body threatened to leap into space

*Jurth shouted to the soldiers, "There he is, paralyzed—grab him!"*

on its own account. King felt knifing pains, a horrible giddiness, and a fear beyond reckoning. Suppose he could not find his way back! Suppose be became an exile from time and space!

*WHEN* his consciousness ceased whirling, he glanced at the dials that recorded the coordinate of the time-space equation. He had gone back, as nearly as he could calculate from old traditions, to the Golden Age, the fabled era before man learned of hate and iron.

War, King had reasoned, was an insane habit that some bird-

brained primitive had devised as a substitute for judgment or intelligence; and thus, a man of the twentieth century, without any illusions as to the glory of strife, might direct the first warrior chief into a happier channel. If these people of the Golden Age, drunk by the novelty of Iron and Power, could see what evolution had finally made of war, they might sober up. War had once been an adventure, but it had long since lost whatever redeeming quality it had possessed.

Through the ports of the time machine, King looked at the green-gold jungles of an infant world. Tall tree ferns trembled in the breeze. The jade waters of a lake lapped a shore fringed with gigantic reeds and grasses; bright insects flashed gold and crimson.

King opened the hatch and stepped to the springy turf. Ages were not as sharply divided as political boundaries, and he would have to reconnoiter to see if he had actually reached the Golden Age.

Then he saw the girl. At the first stirring of the foliage, he had reached for his Colt, not knowing what prehistoric terrors might come out of the jungle; but now his hand dropped. She had the rounded hips and tapered lines of a wood nymph; she moved effortlessly, and the breeze pulled at the translucent tunic that modeled her bosom and the slim curve of her waist. King wondered for a moment if this exquisite creature were just another one of those taunting fancies that had at times crowded equations and integrals from his weary brain.

The girl's blue skirt reached a little below her knees; a costume that reminded him somewhat of the classical drapes worn by women pictured on fragments of Greek pottery. The warm light shaped a golden halo about her head; her unbound hair trailed in copper-colored luxury to her hips.

She started, wide eyed, when she saw King. Impulsively, he came toward her, and said, "Don't be afraid, I'm a stranger and maybe you could tell me where I am."

Her gray-green eyes showed her perplexity, but she smiled, recognizing the friendliness of his voice. King could not understand a word of her answer, but that made little difference; her voice warmed him, and made him forget, the wonder of having traveled all those centuries into time and space. Whatever she had said, she meant that he was welcome. Then, coming within arm's length, he noted that the skirt was torn, and that scratches criss-crossed her calves and thighs. Her tunic was tattered, and her sides were bruised and scarred. He caught her arm and gestured toward the time machine, saying, "You'd better meet the first aid kit."

He could not understand her answer, but there was meaning in the way she fell in step with him, her hip brushing against him, her arm closing against her side and imprisoning the hand he had laid on her elbow. King's blood sang as if it had been blended with the sap of the young earth.

A rosy flush spread over the girl's cheeks when she looked up and saw King's ardent glance. She held up her free hand, and showed him the small band of yellow metal about her wrist. On this curious bracelet were two golden cases, neither of them much larger than a man's watch; a small reel of fine cable connected them. With her other hand she took off one of the cases and slipped it to King's wrist.

*SHE* spoke again, and King could now understand her speech; rather, read her thoughts, in spite of the foreign words.

"I am Ania, a slave, and I ran away from my master, Jurth. He beats me. As you can see—" She half turned, and King saw that her back was seamed with red welts. "He used to be so kind and friendly, like the rest of us. But who are you? I've never seen such strange clothes though they're really becoming."

"I'll give you something to put on those scratches, and while you're doctoring yourself, I'll tell you, though I'm afraid I can't make it very clear. I've come back from what is the future to you; back thirty-two thousand, seven hundred thirteen years—" He lost count of his dial reading, and had to start all over again, for Ania had snuggled up close to him in the cramped cabin of the time cruiser. He finished, "Six months and twenty-two days."

He showed her how to use an iodine swab.

"Oh—that stings! But I can't understand, coming back from the future. It sounds impossible. And why did you do it?"

"We have a disease in our time. A disease called war. Fighting that would be bad enough even if it settled anything, which it never does." He bitterly went on, "Two of my brothers were killed, and a third one is a horrible cripple. I was too young to go. I was sorry then, but when I saw the one who returned, I wished he too had died. So I have come back through time to find the man who started war."

"War!" Ania frowned. "I can say it, but I don't understand."

He was in the golden age; her answer assured him of that. His theory was justified. More than that, her master, Jurth, was strangely and unaccountably becoming vicious.

Jurth, the father of strife? Then this was the dawn of discord!

King caught Ania in his arms. "Tell me about Jurth. I won't let him hurt you."

Ania anxiously asked, "You won't go back into the future without taking me with you?"

"Tell me about Jurth," he evaded, and turned toward the shade of the swaying tree ferns.

There he seated himself on the springy turf and drew in an exhilarating breath. The air of this young world gave him vitality that no human being had had for centuries. He drew Ania closer and kissed her upturned lips; she clung to him, sighed rapturously, and the warmth of her mouth and the pressure of her encircling arms troubled King until there was no room left in his whirling brain for anything but this dawn woman and her possessive beauty.

When King finally got the conversation back to Jurth, Ania explained, "He has studied the forces of nature and bent them to his own use. This thing that makes me understand you—or any other foreigner I might meet—a sort of thought-reading thing, I guess you'd call it, is one of the things Jurth made. But some of his inventions are evil. He makes weapons to kill, to paralyze. Every wise man has servants, lots of them, but Jurth sends out fighting men to take prisoners. That's why he invented this thought-disc, so the strangers could understand his orders."

Pride; greed; restless ambition—this Jurth was moved by the very things that made war. Find Jurth, and give peace to all the centuries to come. For all his horror of killing and wounding, King knew that he had to finish Jurth.

*IN* the meanwhile, the sun was setting, and the time machine, cramped though it was, would be the safest shelter. King rose, gave Ania his hand. "Tomorrow—"

Ania's cry of dismay cut him short. There was a crashing in the brush, and a confusion of deep voices. "That's Jurth!" she cried. "Hurry—before—"

Three men bounded from the edge of the small clearing, and cut off King's retreat to the time machine. The foremost was as tall as King, but heavier of limb and deeper of chest; a black beard jutted aggressively from his craggy face. In one big hand he had a nine-thonged whip. The muscles of his legs and arms were like hawsers. He halted, cracked his scourge, and gestured to Ania. In his other hand he had a rod of bluish metal, tipped with a glass-like bulb; King, taking in the newcomers at a glance, assumed that this was a scepter or other emblem of rank.

Like their chief, Jurth's two retainers wore kilts and short sleeved jackets, but their weapons were three-pronged spears. King jerked clear of Ania's embrace. "Let go! You run to the machine while I stop these fellows!"

He snapped the telepathic coil and cord from his wrist, and thrust the girl from him. He drew the heavy pistol. The two spearmen were easy targets. But something stayed his hand, and he was glad, for an envoy of peace should certainly not shoot men armed with tridents; so he yelled a warning, and gestured, hoping that they would know enough to stop.

Ania, instead of dashing on, had stopped, unwilling to leave King. One of the spearmen swerved and bounded toward her. King fired, purposely throwing the shot against a rock that jutted up out of the turf, right in front of the big fellow's path. Chips of rock peppered his legs. "Halt, or I'll hit you!" King warned.

The man stopped. Then Jurth raised the rod, and King learned that it was more than a scepter. A tongue of light the length of a man's hand flamed from the glass bulb. King's right arm went numb, and his pistol dropped from his grasp. Amazement froze him; be did not know which way to go, or what to do.

Jurth was now upon him, the scourge hissing in a backward arc. King ducked. While his right arm was still useless, his left was unharmed. He came up, bringing one from the turf, and the blow snapped Jurth's head back. But he had an iron jaw, and instead of dropping in his tracks, Jurth bellowed and slashed home again with the short-lashed scourge.

Apparently he forgot his peculiar ray projector, or else the whip suited his mood. He drove King back with cutting lashes; one peeled his ribs, a second crippled his arm to the shoulder.

King took a third blow. He recoiled, raised his arm as if to shield his face, yelled as if in terror. Jurth laughed and wound up for the cut to lay him out. This was what King had expected. He lunged, letting his legs propel him, and with shoulder and one sound arm he caught Jurth below the knees, just as the whip hissed through empty space.

Jurth thumped to the turf. King followed through, booting his oppressor in the pit of the stomach. He had pretty well forgotten his pacific mission. He cut loose and booted his limp opponent another one, and wondered when he had ever had such a pleasant afternoon.

*KING* was about to get up so he could trample Jurth into the ground when a trident prodded his back. The cold metal brought him to his senses. In his fury he had forgotten the spearman and Ania. Now, startled and menaced, he realized what he had been trying to do, and he was ashamed. Not but what Jurth deserved a mauling for whipping a girl like Ania; rather, King felt cheap that ecstasy of rage. Something was undermining his character; he had given up ten years of his life to confer the boon of peace on mankind, and now a slugging match made him drunk with fighting spirit.

The other spearman had caught Ania. Seeing the trident that prodded King's back, she screamed and broke away. Her captor dropped his weapon and bounded after her, before she could snatch the other spearman's trident. He caught her shoulder, tore her tunic to the waist, and then made another lunge. This time he got her about the waist. Kicking and screaming, clawing and wriggling, Ania ended up with little more than a scrap of skirt and her ruddy hair to cover her. She went limp; her captor grinned, wiped the sweat from his forehead—and then Ania broke loose, and dashed for the time machine.

She had not the faintest idea of how to work it, but a struggle in the instrument compartment could disturb almost any combination of levers and start it off, marooning King in the dawn of discord, and carrying Ania and one of her assailants into the twentieth or any other century, past or future. Terror made King move without thought. He yelled and bounded forward, and the spearman at his back was so startled that for an instant, he did not thrust.

King had no time to retrieve his pistol. He outran the spearman, and overtook Ania's pursuer. He tackled the fellow from the side, and sent him smashing against the trunk of a tree fern. That settled him. "Ania, get in!" King panted, and clawed at a rock, "while I finish this other fellow." He tore the rock from its bed of moss, and again the fine fury of the young world intoxicated him. He crouched near the hatch of the time machine, ready to heave the heavy missile. His lips were drawn back; his teeth showed.

The spearman backed away. He was afraid of a twentieth century pacifist. And then Jurth rolled over on his face and got to his knees. He roared, leveled his scepter. King sidestepped, but he was too slow. There was a momentary spurt of flame, and King's legs froze, his whole side and arm went dead, and he toppled over with his missile.

His brain had been touched by this last blast, and while he was not wholly unconscious, he was in a dreamlike haze. He knew only that they were carrying him past a lake, through a jungle, up a mountain. His wits receded, letting him into blackness, and when they returned, he saw a little of his approach to a gray granite fortress whose turrets reached into the clouds.

*WHEN* King's scrambled senses at last got in step with each other, he was lying on a low couch, and looking through a window which pierced a thick stone wall. A lock clicked, and he sat up. Jurth was coming through a narrow doorway; after him came a dark woman whose beauty was marred by her sullen mouth and stormy eyes.

Her hair had the sheen of a black panther's coat, and her lips were full and luscious as the tawny curves that rounded out the bodice of her silken gown. King was fascinated by the sway of her hips, by the sudden brightening of her black eyes. On one wrist she had the telepathic device, one of whose units she unclasped as she came closer. Her perfume stirred King's blood, and he forgot both Ania and his purpose in traveling back into the remote past.

Jurth remained in the doorway for a moment, then he retreated, closing the door. The dark woman knelt beside King, so close that her shapely body pressed against him; her fingertips were caressing as she fastened the golden clip on his wrist, soft and smooth as her speech. Her voice was like deep piled velvet, persuasive as her perfume.

"I am Foma, one of Jurth's discarded wives," she purred, "and on the pretext of helping him, I came to help you, Man-From-Times-To-Come. You are in Jurth's palace, high above the great city, Jhaggar, the city older than time. Now Jurth could see that you are stubborn and hard-willed and that he could not win the truth from you with any torture short of killing you, so he depends on me to persuade you to speak. But I can help you, and I will. For all his wisdom, there are things that Jurth does not understand."

Even a scientist would not be ignorant of the wiles of a jealous woman; but King was not certain that Foma actually would help him outwit Jurth, so he said, guardedly, "I am an explorer, seeking the beginning and the end of time. I seek nothing hut wisdom."

"Nothing but wisdom?" Her arms slipped about him, and her question ended in the ardent pressure of her lips. "The slave girl told us of your coming out of the future. You could go back into the future, you and I. Take me with you and I'll help you get to your time machine."

Apparently Ania had not spoken of his mission to end war. Perhaps she had feigned ignorance, and Jurth had guessed the nature of the machine.

*He made another lunge,*
*and this time he got*
*her about the waist.*

"Nothing but wisdom," King repeated, though his heart was pounding so that he could hardly speak, and the dark woman's insistent lips were dizzying his judgment and resolution. "And when I return—"

Foma's eager embrace made the contact clip slip from King's wrist, and he could not understand her words; but there was no need of speech.

Later, Foma left the cell; the door opened when she tapped,

and King saw the guards posted in the hall. Presently she returned with a tray heaped with roasted meat and ripe fruit that was not quite like any King had ever seen; a golden flagon and golden goblets gleamed from the tray.

She poured an amber-colored wine whose fragrance was as rich as her own perfume, and as he ate, she pillowed her lustrous head against his shoulder. "You don't trust me," Foma reproached. "You are afraid of Jurth, because he and his men handled you roughly, thinking you were a foreigner who had tempted one of his slaves to run away. But he is not really such a violent person. He's keeping you prisoner simply to learn more of the future from which you come."

**STRAIGHT** thinking was difficult with Foma's curves pressed so close to him, but King resisted the urge to kiss her upturned lips. "For a discarded favorite, you're making a good case for him!"

"You could pretend to tell him the truth, pretend to demonstrate and explain. Otherwise, I don't know how you'll ever get out of here. How can you get to your time machine!"

"You can find a way," King said, evading her tightening embrace. "Tell Jurth I'm still suspicious of you and everyone."

Her eyes gleamed wrathfully when he thrust her away. He was glad, for that one betraying flash of anger told him how narrowly he had missed taking her into his confidence. Then she shrugged, and went to the door; the guards let her out, and bolts slid into place.

King had little time to plan any escape from a cell whose window was so far above the courtyard that only a bird could have left. The clang of iron startled him, and that angry ring shocked him more than the face of the man who entered: Jurth had returned.

*Iron:* a rarity, used only by Jurth's guard: everything else was of gold, but the golden age was fading, and the iron age was starting. The ancient myths had been more than lovely legends; they were history dimmed by years.

A squad of guards was at Jurth's back. At his gesture, they

swooped around on both sides, seizing King before he could begin to resist. By sheer weight and strength, they subdued his struggles, and stretched him flat on the hard stones. Jurth knelt and clipped the telepathic speech transmitter to King's wrist. That done, he drew from his belt a small cylinder with a long, fine needle at one end. With the plunger at the other, it seemed very much like a surgeon's hypodermic. But Jurth's smile made it a fearsome weapon.

"Man of the Future, you are subtle and hard-willed! Foma has kissed the truth out of many men, and seeing you and Ania, I was sure Foma would not fail. But since you are tough as iron, the sacred metal, I will give you something that melts iron unless you tell me why you came back from the future. How do you operate the machine! Tell me, or—"

"Try and make me tell!" To be marooned in the fading years of the Golden Age would be pleasant, but King shuddered at the thought of a savage like Jurth going into the future to make it worse than it actually was. "Kill me if you want, but I won't tell you. Not until I am ready!"

The descending needle stopped an inch from King's chest. Jurth said, "Not until you are ready... well... this may hasten you."

King flinched when the needle sank deep into his flesh; but when Jurth pressed the plunger, sharp agony spread from the puncture and raced through his nerves. His groans made the vault echo; the guards could hardly hold him flat. Jurth snarled, "Steady, you fools! If he drives this in too deep, it'll kill him and you'll wish it had killed you!"

The agony radiated; it was as if King's body were filled with a searing network of electric wires, torturing every nerve. Fire and acid poured through his veins; he could taste the metallic venom in his mouth, he could smell it in his nostrils. His eyes stared through a haze of changing colors. Guards came running from the hall to help those who could hardly restrain the writhing madman.

Finally, King would have spoken. He knew that he was beaten, but he could not speak. His outraged nerves collapsed and his body with them. The telepathic disc had been displaced during

*She descended, swung in and missed, swung in again.*

his last struggle, and thus Jurth did not suspect how close he had been to victory. He rose, gestured to his retainers, and stalked toward the door.

King, partially regaining consciousness, understood the derisive gesture. It meant, "There is more. I can give more than you can take."

**THE** sun was setting when the door opened again, and Foma returned. In the ruddy light he saw the dark bruises on her shoulders, the welts that criss-crossed her legs, and showed dimly through the frail cloth of her gown. She ran toward him, without any studied gait or gesture; she was in his arms before he could sit up or inquire, and as she pressed her lips to his, she snapped the clip on his wrist.

"Look—he beat me for failing. I was going to trick you—you were right—but he has beaten me once too often—we'll kill him—and we'll escape into the future—"

She poured it out in a gasp. This could be part of a trick, but the passionate intensity of her voice, the tremor of her body, the insistence of her grasp, these all convinced King. Where before he had sensed a studied cunning, now he felt that a primitive creature revealed herself without reservation.

Her fury for a moment terrified him. Unalloyed, primal rage, a slaying lust: the same ferocity that Ania had described, a new mood and one foreign to that idyllic world until Jurth had delved too deeply into wisdom, and his pride had made him greedy and grasping.

This woman, tainted by Jurth's contagious wrath, would doom the man who was the root of discord. King was more and more pleased by the need of killing Jurth. He knew that he also was succumbing to the murderous vibration with which Jurth made raiders and slayers of his once kindly followers, but this no longer shocked him.

Foma read his thought, and curled up in his arms.

"We'll be happy in the future," she sighed, languidly....

*IN* the days that followed, King saw Jurth's army drilling in the court: fifty men, practicing parries and thrusts with a newly invented weapon that looked like a cross between a scythe and a pike. On other days they marched out, and King saw red against the sky, the flare of burning villages. Then, captives; the capital was growing from these new additions, and Jhaggar's outskirts reached further and further beyond the original walls.

At first the natives were bewildered. Some tried to share the burdens that the newcomers carried: others hospitably offered the newly captured prisoners cups of wine, but soon they learned to avoid such unpatriotic gestures. Before King had been a captive for many weeks, the natives of Jhaggar were hurling rocks, shaking fists, jeering at the prisoners.

Down in the streets, King saw a modification of the telepathic disc. There was no longer any interlinking cord, and only the slaves wore them. This was a great improvement, for with hordes of foreigners dragged into town by Jurth's ever increasing army, the taskmasters could not possibly have used the old system of communication.

King, kept from torture because Jurth was too busy with war, was biding his time. Foma's visits convinced him that she did have a bitter grudge against Jurth, who had discarded her in favor of a lovely captive. From her, he learned the language, and he questioned the guards about Ania, but with no result. Once, however, he caught a glimpse of her in the corridor, and he was certain that she had seen him.

Late one night the hall door opened and Foma hurried in, with a faint tinkling of anklets and rustling of silk. Her hand trembled as she caught his shoulder. "John-king, I have found out—it is in the main laboratory—under lock—Jurth has the key—"

King drew her closer, felt her violent heartbeat, and the warmth of her mouth as she returned his kiss; but she broke away, saying, "It is different, this time. I told him how stubborn you are. So you will be tortured to the extreme. You must escape. Tonight—when he returns from operating the vibration-thing that makes people eager to fight."

"Get that key—I'll take you with me!" He meant it, for though he was hungry for the sight of Ania, he could not abandon Foma to Jurth's fury. "But the guards?"

"We have another new custom," she explained. "Giving-gifts-to-turn-away-from-duty."

"We have a shorter word for that," King said.

**DURING** his captivity, King had felt the operation of the war-vibration machine. The faint, hateful humming was bad enough, after an hour; but there was apparently some ultrasonic pulsation that aroused fighting fury. His only hope was in the fact that Jurth seemed to need this vibrational irritant to get his people aroused to the right degree of patriotism. So there was hope: destroy the machine whose damnable impulses had poisoned the whole race; had started a cycle of slaying, of destroying the peaceful, until the breed of the twentieth century could by a few newspaper headlines be whipped to insane fury.

Even as he pondered on it, the baleful humming began. He got up and paced the floor, his jaw set, his eyes narrowed; and for lack of anything more definite, he cursed Foma for taking so long about her arrangements. He pounded the door and shouted at the guards. They answered him with like contempt. One said, "I'm sick of watching that fellow. I've a notion to spear him and settle this business."

The other said, "I've been thinking of that—but we better wait—"

"Wait, my eye!"

King taunted them so they would come in to try to kill him. He seized the metal-framed couch and carried it across the cell, ready to heave against their shins when they came in. The hate machine was whipping up a vortex of rage. Down below, the city began to mutter; riots were breaking out, and zealous watchmen were clubbing or spearing citizens into order.

Some master raid must be in the making. King began to think of Jurth, but just for the general purpose of killing him. In his fine fury, he had no purpose or aim. And he hated Ania. Damn her spineless soul, all honey and kisses, and had she ever tried to help him!

Then, behind him, King heard the mellow ring of gold. The goblet he had set on the sill was now rolling across the floor. Tiny feet and shapely calves were silhouetted against the moonlight; a woman was sliding down a rope that apparently came from a window still higher in the turret. Curiosity, and the woman's breathtaking peril made King forget his fury.

The skirt hitched up, up, up as she descended, swung in and missed, swung in again, and then got her bare feet on the deeply recessed sill. But before she arched her supple body enough to back from the sill into the cell, King knew that Ania had finally found her way to him.

Breathless, she clung to him, and it was more her gesture than her words that made him understand when she took a key from her bosom. "All these weeks—the time machine—now we can escape—before that awful woman comes back—"

"So you know—?"

"I don't care; she forced herself on you!"

Ania turned to the sill. "I can't climb up, it was bad enough sliding down. But you're strong, John-king, and I'll wait for you to get around to the door and let me out. There are new guards; the old ones go out to war."

King was so glad that not even the hammering waves of hatred could make him warlike.

Then the climb. In the interests of science, he had kept fit, with road work and gymnasium, in that dim future which none of those about him could even picture. Now he needed his training, every bit of it, as he went up, hand over hand. The hard twisted cord cut his palms. He should have removed his boots, but in his excitement he had overlooked that handicap.

*ANIA* had slipped through the upper window easily enough; for all her shapeliness, she was slender. It had never occurred to her that King's worst struggle would be at the narrow slot that pierced the masonry. His arms were wooden, his palms were drenched with sweat, his legs had no resiliency left. The terror of that deep gulf had tightened him, exhausted him, made it as if he had climbed twice as far. For minutes he lay there, wedged in that narrow slot, not in any danger of sliding back, but certain that if he had to retreat, his strength would not permit him to slip down the cord and back to his prison.

He was close to the hate vibration. The masonry shivered in resonance with its pulse. Again King felt the whip of wrath. He lurched, bruised and cut himself, wedged tight; but now reckless, he snarled with an insane anger against even himself, and somehow he tore loose, and dropped in a heap on the floor of the uppermost hall.

Then King heard Jurth's bull-roar and a woman's scream. A whip crackled. As King dashed down the hall, Jurth snarled and cursed Foma, threatened her with all known tortures if she did not return the key she had stolen.

The laboratory was in the cross passage at King's right. He rounded the corner and saw Jurth and Foma in front of the locked door. Her tawny body gleamed in the light of the torches whose cold flame lined the hall. Jurth's whip had peeled most of the gown from her back. When she flung herself at him, screaming and clawing, he slapped her with the flat of his hand. She stumbled and fell in a heap against the wall.

"Where's that key!" Jurth roared, flicking the whip.

King darted in. This blow had to be good—and it was good. Jurth, question frozen on his lips, toppled to the floor. He was so stiff that he did not make any instinctive move to break his fall.

King jerked Foma to her feet and hustled her to the laboratory door. He ignored her question as to his escape and his possession of the key. It fitted the lock. He booted the panel open, and spent a moment looking and thinking.

There were coils and alembics, the strange devices which in some ways were primitive, in other ways far advanced of twentieth century instruments; at a glance, he sensed that many of the arts he knew had never been known to the ancients, and that on the other hand a wealth of science had been lost, hopelessly perhaps, in thirty thousand odd years.

Looking and thinking. There was his time machine. There was the war vibrator whose infra-sonic humming made the room shiver. It had dials and levers and controls, it had focused projectors, traversing wheels; its concentration could be turned in every direction. King saw this, saw all these other things, and wondered whether he should escape, or whether he should patch up a truce with Jurth and finally go back into the twentieth century with a full knowledge of all the lost arts.

But how to get Ania! Only Foma could enter the cell, or pass the guards.

"Jurth is going to stay unconscious for some time. Run down and get—" He fumbled at his belt. "My pistol."

That was a bad guess. Foma's eyes hardened and her lips curled. "You're trying to trick me! You know you never had those belt-weapons in your cell. There they are—see them—"

He followed her gesture. His pistol was on a bench, apparently ready for an examination Jurth had not yet had time to make. If that demon learned the power of gunpowder! Horror drove King across the laboratory for his weapon.

"How did you get that key!" Foma screamed, dashing after him. "Sending me on a crazy chase—when you had it—trying to get rid of me—after I've been beaten on your account—oh, I know, it's that Ania, that slave girl, that—no wonder she's been playing up to Jurth. You fool, he'll kill her when he finds out!"

He caught her by the shoulders. "Shut up! Shut up!" She thought he was merely trying to sidetrack her; Foma did not realize that Ania was in King's cell, waiting for release. "Wait a second—no, come with me; there are things I have to get. We'll need them in the future."

The war machine's devilish vibration was whipping King to wrath, and it stirred Foma's sultry temper. If either had been calm, the impending rage would have drowned in reason, but as it was, she believed nothing that he said. She shrieked, "You'll not go down, you'll not desert me, you'll not get her!"

"Shut up!" King slapped her; she tumbled end for end, cracked her head against the wall and lay there, moaning.

He had to kill the guards or he could not get Ania, and he needed a weapon. He dashed about the spacious laboratory and found one of the axes that Jurth was perfecting. He snatched it from the bench, whirled it. His legs had limbered up again, and he could settle any two soldiers who had ever lived! He'd chop Jurth lengthwise and crosswise on the way down to get the guards! He spun, eyed the war-vibrator: ought to chop that to pieces; that was Jurth's work. He hated everything that made him think of Jurth.

*THEN* his frenzy of plans was scrambled by surprise. He had fate in his hands, he had the power to change every day of the following thirty odd thousand years; but only a god could have done the right thing at the right time.

He paused to buckle on his gun. Something compelled that. Oh, of course, mustn't leave any specimen of gunpowder for Jurth to analyze. Then he heard Ania's voice from the doorway: "John-king! I bribed the guard—I'm free!"

King lowered the axe. "There it is!" He pointed at the time machine. "Get in, I've got to see a man out in the hall!"

*KILL* Jurth; to wreck the war vibrator would only make him invent another one. King was confused by the number of things he had to do. He felt that he must hurry, lest enraged fate destroy a man who upset thirty thousand years of history.

Kill Jurth. Then he saw Foma was on her feet. She tugged at a lever, and a great gong rolled and boomed. On the floor just below, men shouted, armor clanged. The guard was turning out. Kill Foma! An insane thing to do, but King was dizzy with hate. Stupefied by his own fury, he stood there, and neither struck Foma nor ran into the hall to finish Jurth.

Foma bounded to the time machine, screaming. Ania, gentle Ania bounded out to meet her; eyes green with rage, nails raking, teeth exposed, she closed in with Foma. The war vibrator had been too much for her, and she knew all about the dark woman's love for King.

White limbs and tawny, flailing and threshing; brunette with fresh nail marks, blonde with darkening bruises, a tangle of hair and shredded garments. King shouted, "Stop it, you fools. I'll take you both!"

He went to shake sense into them, and dropped the axe. Already, the guards were clanging up the stairway into the hall. And Jurth was bellowing. Shaken by his ever quickening sense of nightmare failure, King picked up the axe. Jurth dropped his whip, and reached for the ray-scepter. King hurled the ponderous axe.

A good throw, but not quite good enough. It made Jurth shake his head. The glancing axe-head hit into the masonry, sparks flew, and the weapon clanged against the opposite wall. Jurth leveled the paralyzer. King ducked. The struggling girls rolled against his calves; he tumbled over them, backwards in a heap.

Jurth shouted to the soldiers, "There he is, paralyzed! Grab him!"

The column of fours came pounding in, tridents leveled. King whirled to seize Ania. But she was locked in Foma's grip; the brunette, catching the full blast of the power that would have paralyzed King had he not tripped, could not let go of her rival. King could not pry them apart, nor lift the two; not through that narrow hatch.

The ray projector blazed again, the heads of the guards, who ran at a crouch. Panic drove King into the time machine. He pulled the hatchway. The blast was wasted on massive metal, and tridents vainly chipped at the port covers and the walls. He thrust the reverse lever home, pushed the starter.

The howling soldiers blurred in a gray haze. When King's senses became normal again, he was in his own laboratory, and not showing any sign of battering or struggle. But he was not quite the same. He stared at the emptiness between the two hands he held just far enough apart to have pressed the curve of a slender girl's waist. He shook his head, and hated himself.

Outside, newsboys called war extras. He had failed because he had been incited by the same fury he had gone out to destroy. But since the Golden Age people had succumbed to the hate wave, how could he, with the heritage of a thousand warring generations, have resisted it! He let his empty hands meet, and closed his eyes.

No man can alter that which has been, he now realized; inevitably, he could not have brought either Ania or Foma back into this century. But he had brought back a memory, and Ania's loveliness blossomed in his fancy. And he thought of Foma as a sense-stirring fragrance, an ardor whose very reflection made him restless.

He went out to eat. He could not believe his watch. Allowing for his period of bewilderment, it seemed that no time had been consumed. His shirt, all torn, could have been damaged by his involuntary struggle against fading consciousness.

An illusion! Then it had in some way given him peace, and the knowledge that no man can undo what has been done. That scent in his nostrils... go out, it told him, look around... that fragrance had come from no laboratory....

Then he saw the girl, blonde and slender and shapely; the breeze whipped a print skirt against her lovely legs, and tugged at her shimmering hair. Something about her walk made him think of Ania, and so did her profile. Her side glance and her almost-smile. He knew that he would soon meet her, and find what he had almost brought from the dawn of discord.

As King watched the setting sun play tricks with the girl's skirt, he knew that scientific experiments do have practical results. If she had not reminded him of Ania, he'd never have looked long enough to want to follow her....

# The Old Gods Eat

*In this loneliest corner of Cornwall no one ever left except those who disappeared. A monster was eating the peasants, and when Dale investigated he found a girl who showed him things about the mystery— and he found a horror that he hadn't suspected....*

*W*HEN THE 5:37 stopped at Pengyl, I wasn't surprised to see I was the only passenger who got off at that clutter of old masonry houses with thatched roofs; this was the loneliest corner of Cornwall. No one ever arrived there, and no one ever left, except those who disappeared, which was the business that brought me from London. A monster was eating the peasants, Anyway, that was what Lord Treganneth said in his letter.

A fifteen-year-old Rolls Royce pulled up, and a big man got out. His face was as rugged as the Cornish coast: heavy chin, broad mouth, jutting nose; and his shaggy tweeds made him look even rougher. He said, brusquely, "I'm Treganneth, You're Mr. Dale, I fancy?"

His voice had a rumble like the surf that was shaking the ground under my feet and filling the air with fine spray. What a place! Even the sea hated it and tried to pound it to pieces.

If he wanted to be superior, okay; his cheek for twenty guineas, a hundred bucks in American money, made him a nice guy.

I heaved my bag into the car. He said, "Get in the back seat." Then he took the wheel. That was funny. It made no sense, an earl or something of the sort not having a chauffeur. I wondered for a second or two whether the monoceros had eaten all the servants.

Judging from the coat of arms on Treganneth's stationery, a monoceros is a kind of a sea monster with a horn like a unicorn; a seagoing dragon with a long spike coming out between his eyes. The motto on the engraving was funny, too: WE SERVE THE MONOCEROS.

In the couple minutes I'd waited in Pengyl, I figured that it was a ghost town. Now I began to see the people, and I wondered where they'd been up till the time Treganneth drove up.

A man in an oilskin coat and hat shook his fist from a doorway. Before we reached the edge of the village, another man popped out. He heaved a cobble stone and yelled, "Where's Harry Penfield, you bloody—?"

The rock smashed against the door. A bit higher, and it'd have knocked Treganneth from the wheel. This struck me as an odd way to treat the earl who owns the country for miles around. Maybe that was why he had sent for me, an American.

I had a sort of reputation wished on me.

*I'D* come to London to nail an embezzler; bonding company business, you know. The gent couldn't run further, so he hung himself with the cord of his bath robe. The papers made a play of me hounding the man to his death. That must have pleased Treganneth, so here I was.

A rock crashed against the rear quarter. Another knocked out the rear glass, though no pieces hit me. The people did not like Treganneth.

Cornish miners are the best in the world, I've heard, and the most superstitious: too many generations under ground, and the earth whispered to them. And the fishermen are as bad. Whether Treganneth did or did not have a monster around his castle, the peasants all thought he had.

We climbed a brisk grade and got up through the mist. I was almost shocked to see how much light there was, for I'd gotten the feeling that the sun never shone here. A gray masonry fortress loomed up from a hill; it had a castellated turret, with little windows out through thick walls. For all the light, the place made me think of a second hand coffin.

"Hold it!" I said to Treganneth. "I want to look from here. If there is funny work, whoever does it is leaving trails. The monoceros comes out of the castle and goes over the hills, or the natives go over the hills to the castle. Like in France, aviators used to spot batteries because some dumb artilleryman cut across a meadow."

Treganneth pulled up, but did not answer; he just sat there. I dug into my bag and got out a pair of highpower glasses. Anyone used to ordinarily fine glasses would never imagine how these binoculars gathered light. This time they surprised me; that was when I saw the girl in the turret.

She was gripping the bars, and her face was pressed against the metal. A blanket was over her shoulders. That was all she wore, and it covered her back. She was high-breasted, and her waist was slim, and her hips had a luscious flare. The sill reached up high enough to block observations on her legs and so forth, but I was ready to okay her from the sample displayed. Judging from the way she pressed against the bars she gripped, she was a prisoner.

Lucky she moved away before his lordship got wise that I wasn't studying hillsides. I said, "No, no signs of trespassers here. But who's Harry Penfield?"

Treganneth started. "The last who vanished."

The road curved, dipped, swooped first inland, then along the sea; for a few miles, we were further from the castle than we'd been when I got that not-quite-enough of a look at the blonde with the nice curves pressed against the bars. The road became tougher, the crags wilder; the full roar of the sea burst upon us, and spray drenched the car. And then we were heading for the arched gateway of the castle.

*She was there. The unicorn
spike had taken its victim.*

Grass sprouted between the flagstones of the courtyard. The big iron hinges of the door that opened into the donjon were rusty. The whole place was run down. Ivy grew wild, blocking window after window.

**TREGANNETH** pulled up in front of the door. The place looked deserted; it was dusky in the court and dark inside the donjon, and I didn't like it a bit. People that write about sea monsters eating peasants are not what you want to spend the evening with. If it hadn't been for seeing a chance to see a bit more of the blonde girl, I'd have said, "Here's your twenty guineas, my lord, and nuts for you."

I wanted to see more of that dame. She might be locked up, but I understand locks.

The door opened. A woman in a pink gingham house dress stood there with a kerosene lamp. The castle seemed not to be wired for lights, just for death and disappearance.

"Emily, take Mr. Dale's luggage," Treganneth said.

The dark woman set the lamp in a bracket. I said, "Steady, I can juggle it myself."

She had smooth white skin and black hair, and blue eyes that were almost black. Her thick lashes were a sooty smudge along the lids; the people of Cornwall were Kelts, ancient and unmixed. I knew why I grabbed that bag. Not because she was a woman, but because she made me feel like she owned the place, in the sense that any first inhabitant looks and acts that way.

The wind howled into the court, and pulled her dress tight. She had nice legs, a perfect thirty, speaking of age, not measure; ripe for the picking and not picked over enough to he spoiled.

I followed her into the castle and saw that some of the heap had been remodeled maybe a century ago. The paneling of the big living room was oak, all black with smoke. As I followed Emily to my room on the second floor, I shot a look up the staircase that went up into the turret, where the wind was howling, laughing, snarling at the blonde girl. I decided against asking questions about that angle.

Emily pussyfooted around the room, patting things into shape.

I asked, "What is your idea on this monoceros business? I guess you know why I'm here."

She looked up, and from the corners of her eyes. "I can show you a few things he can't. Late tonight, when no one else is awake."

Anyway you took that, the girl was right. "Dinner will be served in an hour. You needn't dress," she added.

The way it turned out, Treganneth didn't come to dinner. I ate alone in that acre of dark dining room; dark, except for the coals on the hearth, and the two candles which whipped and flickered in the drafts. The wind laughed and cried and booooed. Emily served the roast beef, which was perfect; everything else was cooked to death. But the wine was something to write a book about. She poured some Burgundy and said, "His lordship's brother laid this down in 1914, years before he disappeared."

"Huh! Disappeared?"

"Yes. Along with my late husband, Mr. Polgate. The steward."

"The monoceros got 'em!"

"If you stay awake late enough, I'll show you something that will amaze you."

As it was, every time she bent over to fill that big glass she showed plenty. She was good enough for an earl, anywhere you looked.

*IT* was after midnight when Emily tapped on my door. Her hair hung in two thick braids. She wore a nightgown with a low neck yoke and lace panels on each side; it was trimmed with two rosettes placed just right, though what was beneath didn't need markers! Even though she did wear a heavy robe over that gown, it was a treat. "Treganneth is dead drunk," she said.

When I stepped into the hall, the wind sounded as if a woman were crying. Emily carried an old fashioned lantern, which lighted our way down a murky corridor; then came a stairway that led down into the unmodernized part of the castle, the masonry that was a thousand years old, perhaps a lot more.

It was damp and creepy and there was a funny smell; the iodine odor of the waterfront, the rank salt marsh smell of tidal flats. There was dust on the floor, except for a blurred trail, as if something had been dragged. I began to think of Harry Penfield, the last man to disappear. Then Emily led on into an alcove, and at the end she pointed to a ring in the floor.

It was like other rings I'd seen, heavy iron, rusty, anchored by an eyebolt which was sunk in lead poured into a hole in the masonry. She said, "Pull hard, and lift it."

I pulled. There was a screech, and a slab of masonry swung on pivots. Stairs led down, dark and narrow. And that sea smell, way too much of it. I hung back.

A gust of stale air came up and played tricks with Emily's robe.

Holding the lantern up made the neck yoke pull tight, and the rose-colored silk shaped itself about her hips.

"Don't you want to see more!"

I didn't; not of the underground works, that is, but I felt foolish about backing down. "Go ahead," I told her, and she led on, as if she owned the place. By now, I had a hunch that she did own it, and that Treganneth was just a stooge; the earl who could make her a lady if he wanted to.

We came out in a vault hewn from bedrock. In the center was a roughly circular pit perhaps twenty feet across. The coping along its edge was not more than halfway to Emily's knees, and the runway between it and the wall was not over a yard wide. It gave me the creeps, getting so close to that hole in the rock.

Emily sat down on the damp rock, and caught her knees with her clasped hands. She'd given me the lantern; she said, "Sit down, and blow it out." So I joined her on the steps. They were so narrow I had to wedge close against her. This was once that getting a dame alone in the dark was no treat.

This place was so old I could taste the age. Emily's people, the old people, the Druids that used to offer up human sacrifices at Easter and burn prisoners in wicker cages, had built this. Emily was at home here.

I lifted the shade and blew the light out.

"We may have to wait," she whispered, and leaned close. I could feel her breath in my ear and her hair against my cheek. "That shaft reaches down to where the monoceros lived, and died, a thousand years ago. When the Treganneths were Cornish lords, pirates, raiders."

"So it's dead."

"It died, but it is coming to life."

The smell of iodine, of concentrated sea, became stronger: the pit was breathing. A white mist was rising out of the blackness, it was twisting and writhing.

It took a shape the thickness of a hogshead, and Lord knows how long. The head was a dragon's, a dragon with a yard long spike growing out of its forehead. This was the monoceros en-

*She went ahead with the lantern. "Don't you want to see more?" she asked.*

graved on Treganneth's stationery, and on his carnelian ring of old, soft gold.

Up—up—up—reaching out of the pit. Two men were kicking and clawing in its coils. One looked like Treganneth. Emily yeeped and caught me with both arms. She poured herself over me. I sprawled back against the stairs. I tangled up with her bare legs, and then I made a dive for the treads. She went limp, and I caught her.

*IN* the scramble, I got a look back. The thing was pulling back into the pit, and thinning out to a haze, ribbon-thin. Then it was gone. I was sweating, shaking till my teeth clicked. I grabbed

Emily and headed up those stairs, and I didn't stop for the lantern. I reached the head of the stairs long before I had any hope of getting there, and I took a header. Lucky for Emily I twisted as I flopped, or I'd have smashed her flat. As it was, the crash nearly laid me out. And she came to. She moaned, "It's getting worse. It's reaching further each time. It's calling for its prey—get me out of here—"

I fairly dragged her. It's funny, but I headed for my room, as if that were any safer than anywhere else. When I slammed the bolt, I turned around and saw Emily sag at the knees. She keeled over and flopped in the old lounge.

I stumbled after her. "If Treganneth thinks I am hunting that thing, he is nuts! It sounded like some kind of murder racket when he wrote me, someone giving him the runaround to get him out of his castle. But *that*—what's he think I am?"

"He still thinks something human is tricking villagers into the caves under the castle and killing them. He doesn't know of this place. Promise me you won't tell him. He's so worried now, a shock would drive him mad."

A fellow can't believe everything he sees. Look at that Hindu rope trick. And the little green men a friend of mine used to see in his room. He threw things at them, only they just weren't there. Neither was that monster.

"Okay, I won't tell him. But how did you find that awful place?"

"My late husband, Mr. Polgate, was steward. He used to tell me things. About subcellars of this castle. Then he and the present earl's brother vanished, and no one ever found their bodies. Seven years passed; they were declared legally dead, and I became a legal widow. Jasper—the present earl—came from Australia to take his heritage. And then things happened. Villagers disappeared. People whispered about the monoceros and brought up that old legend of how the Treganneths traced their descent from it."

What she meant was, it was a sort of totem, like the Indians have wolves, bear, and the like for clan ancestors. She went on, "The ancient Treganneths sacrificed captives to the monster, to keep their luck in war. It lived in that pit. It came in from the sea for its offerings. Then an earthquake blocked the passage, and the thing starved when the Treganneths could not find enough victims."

"And now the ghost of the monoceros is eating!"

Now that I'd quieted down a bit, I began to think, "That was malarkey. I didn't see it; it was hypnotism. Decaying sea stuff, phosphorescent vapors, and me thinking about the monoceros ever since I got the earl's cockeyed letter."

I turned to Emily. "Why don't you check out?"

"I belong to the place."

"I don't. I'm a detective. I brought embezzlers from Algiers. From Honduras. But a monoceros is something else. You can keep it."

As a matter of fact, I was getting sore at myself for having gone hog wild down there, but I was giving Emily a line to see what she'd do. There was a trick somewhere.

Emily jumped up, and before I could get a lamplight view of this and that, she had me with both arms. She squeezed close, and not just with her arms, either. "You must stay—you've got to—for *my* sake!"

I was getting high blood pressure from that armful of woman, but I could still add things up. Emily's gown had store folds in it. I noticed that when the robe fell from one shoulder. A brand new gown like that cost a couple guineas; a damn funny expenditure when the earl drove his own fifteen-year-old bus. And she'd lied when she said she and the earl were alone here. How about the blonde gal in the tower!

I played the sap on purpose. I nudged her toward the door. "You're too scared to know what you're talking about. Come back when the monoceros business is settled and see if I head you for the door."

The smile over her shoulder was one of those promises only a chump expects a dame to keep.

The more I thought about the monoceros, as I sat there by the grate, the more I said, "Hell, you do it with mirrors."

*AN* hour passed. Then another. I dug up my flashlight and I put on some felt slippers. It was dark as a squaw's pocket out in that hall. The wind made dirty sounds and ghastly sounds, and then it laughed whenever I jerked back, figuring something was prowling around in the dark. But I got to the stairs that reached up into the hell-blackness of that turret.

By the time I had convinced myself that the monoceros was something I had eaten, I was up as far as the second narrow slot in the two-foot-thick masonry. The moon was full. The crags were shining from spray, and spray jumped up from the roaring sea. If anything was creeping over those hills, it was belly flat.

Then I looked toward the sea again. Something was moving, something white against the dark crags. I knew it was a woman before I could see the curves that made everything certain except her face.

If she wore anything, it wasn't enough to register at night. She was white and shining, and her golden hair rippled in the wind. A man was stumbling over the rocks, waving his arms.

He was gaining. Then she danced ahead and won a length. Then they both were blotted out by a black tongue.

To think that I could dash down stairs and over wet rocks in time to keep the guy from overtaking the girl was crazy, but I was on the way. There is something about a scenario like that that makes a fellow want to keep the other fellow from getting familiar with the girl in question, even if she is a stranger.

When I got there, I saw neither girl nor man. Just wet rocks. Cornwall was where King Arthur got his start, where Merlin did his stuff, where the Lady of the Lake used to hang out. The whole Cornish coast is wacky. The only way to keep from going nuts is not to believe anything you see. But even so, I went back to the turret to find out if there really was a blonde there.

I got my kit of lock picks to work. I'd become handy that way because it simplifies the business of snooping on embezzlers. The door opened easy.

The girl wasn't asleep. She was so scared when the door opened that she couldn't yeep. Moonlight reached into the turret and picked out her beautiful legs, the fine curve of throat and cheek.

I said, "It's all right. If you're a prisoner, maybe I can help you."

"Why didn't you knock, warn me—who are you—?"

I could see her knees shaking, where they peeped out from the gray woolen blanket she clutched to her breast. "I'm Jim Dale, monoceros hunter, and I saw you through the window this afternoon, looking out."

She gasped.

"With glasses. What is the idea, no clothes!"

The flashlight made it clear she didn't have a stitch in the whole turret, just the cot and the blankets.

"I'm Jasper Treganneth's secretary—I mean, I was, when he was in Perth. I followed him when he came to the title. Just imagine, came to this ruin. I was stranded. When my funds were gone, I came to the castle."

"After you'd sold your shoes and clothing for subsistence while job hunting," I cracked, "you came to hide in Treganneth Castle. What was the name, please?"

She flared. "I'm Diane Rolley!"

Then she doubled up and began crying. I sat down on the cot beside her and slipped an arm about her. "Buck up, Diane. I'm a detective, trying to settle this monoceros business. How did you get up here?"

"Jasper locked me up."

"What for?"

She'd let the blanket slip a bit, and for all her trying to cover up with a jerk, I saw enough to prove Treganneth was crazy! Diane said, "This gossip, these disappearances, it was driving me mad. When I decided to go, he wouldn't let me."

"Huh?"

"He was afraid I'd never come back, that I'd spread wild stories about the place, perhaps have him declared insane. He said that if I stayed until things were cleared up, he'd marry me, even though he did have a title and I was a former employee."

*THAT* made sense, but not this business of taking her clothes. When I asked about that, she said, "Just suppose someone did break in and find me; he and that woman could say that I got violent, tore my clothes to shreds. That they kept me here because he didn't want to send me to a madhouse."

Having an audience, even a stranger, made Diane crack. She hung herself around my neck and sobbed, "Get me out of here. Get a closed car. Take me out by night. The villagers would stone me, throw me into the sea, tear me to pieces. They blame me for these deaths. They'll storm the castle if this keeps up."

After what I'd seen of a blonde girl being chased along the cliffs, I could understand why people might pick on Diane.

Well, Diane did persuade me to stick around and plan for her escape, though I insisted on finishing the monoceros business first. But I didn't wait until sunrise. Having cried out her worries, she curled up and went to sleep. The way it was, if I made an immediate getaway, I'd never learn about that ghost monster. The more I saw of this, the more I was sure they did it with mirrors, and I was sore, being played for a chump.

But before I tiptoed out, I did things to the lock. They passed Diane's grub through a wicket, so it was a ten to one shot no one would notice the lock was gummed up.

Early in the morning, Emily brought me a pitcher of hot water; the castle didn't have running water, believe it or not. "Did you sleep well!"

"Lonesome, but otherwise okay. How's the earl, sobered up?"

Treganneth was red eyed. "Didn't want to talk at night. Man's too credulous at night."

We tied into a kidney pie and some bloaters and some porridge. I listened to his yarn about the monoceros. It checked with Emily's account. He made no mention of vaults under the castle except to say, "Blasted nonsense, reptile cult of my ancestors. But the villagers are getting nasty. I want you to explain the disappearances."

"Suppose I inquired around the village?"

"My good man, I disclaim any liability if you get your skull cracked. After what happened yesterday, I have no intention of returning to Pengyl."

"Let me drive your car. How about the keys?"

Treganneth said, "Emily will drive to market. Go with her."

He rose and headed for the study. I was thoroughly dismissed.

*GOING* to market in Pengyl wasn't fun, Someone heaved a cobblestone at the car and an old hag screeched, "Where's that golden-haired witch? Bring her out!"

Emily leaned out. The men who had rocks dropped them. The old woman stopped cursing and muttering. The men said. "We chucked 'em before we saw it was you. But you better not go back."

Emily pulled up. A crowd gathered. An ugly crowd of gnarled old people. There weren't more than half a dozen young men, and girls were even scarcer. A beak-nosed fellow said, "Ye better not go back. Lon Wellman hasn't come home, and we know he ain't coming back; they never come back. Before God, we're going to tear that place stone from stone, Mis' Polgate, and you're one of us. We don't want you hurt, but there's no saying what people do when they go mad."

That wasn't all. There was that man chasing that blonde girl. Out of the chatter, I got it: a golden-haired witch luring young men to the monoceros. Some of these folks had a funny way of saying witch, I guess it was the Cornwall accent or something. It would be bad if they got hold of Diane.

We went to the market. On the way back, I asked Emily, "What's this golden-haired… uh, witch business, the earl held out on me, and so did you?"

"That would have distracted you from the monoceros. These young men are mortally afraid, but each one brags about a blonde girl from London or somewhere spending a weekend at the sea, and being impressed by him and coming back to meet him. Women—young and attractive women—are scarce—" She sighed. "As scarce as young and attractive men. Oh, what a God forsaken edge of nowhere this is!"

"So they sneak out to meet the blonde baby, making a careful sneak so none of the other boys cut in, and—one more lad fades?"

Emily nodded. "The fourth. Or fifth. A witch tempting them into the den of the monoceros. You know how such a story spreads."

When we got back to the castle, Treganneth called me into his study. It was an old, dark room, all lined with old, leather-bound books in oak cases. He had some of them spread out on the big table, and there was a square of parchment written in jet black ink.

His hand shook when he pointed, and so did his voice: "Dale, I've been finding old records. The way to get to the foundations of this place. There is a crypt. There was a monster, centuries ago, and it did live on human sacrifices the heathen Treganneths offered, long before King Arthur's time. It's utter rubbish, but here is something strange—here was a golden haired witch who lured victims to the monoceros, once the Treganneths turned against the Druids and became Christians."

"You believe that?"

"I don't know what I believe."

"Another man vanished, last night."

Treganneth groaned, passed one hand before his eyes. "Again!"

I prodded him. He straightened up.

"You're holding out. I want the straight of it, or you can chase yourself."

He got haughty and tough. "What do you mean?"

"Emily Polgate has a hold on you."

He wouldn't say yes, and he wouldn't say no; he just glared. I took another crack at him: "When we stopped on the ridge and I took out my binoculars. I got a good look at the girl in the turret. Who is the girl, and why!"

Treganneth jumped up, sweating. "Why—you insolent puppy!"

"Take it easy. The first thing you know, the yokels are going to take this place to pieces by hand and then take blondie to pieces and Emily, and you too. What kind of a game is this, you having a dame trapping yokels? Monster, my eye; the chumps fall over the cliff, the waves pound them to pulp."

Treganneth was white now, and his heavy jaw twitched. "The girl in the tower—she's there for her own good. She's quite mad."

"How about you and Emily Polgate?"

"I prefer not to discuss that."

"Emily has loyally held down the fort, then hell pops; all the servants check out, men disappear. All of them young men."

"For God's sake, shut up! Let's look into this crypt. Show it is empty. Throw the place open to the villagers."

*TREGANNETH* took the chart and a flashlight. In a few minutes, we were in that dark tangle of vaults and passages. He hunted a few minutes in the blind alley, and then he saw the trap with the ring.

The smell of iodine, of sea decay came swooping up. We went down the narrow stairs, Treganneth was a lord, all right. He led the way. That made me feel better. I didn't want him in back of me.

At the bottom of the stairs, he saw the lantern, and pulled up sharp. "By Jove! Someone's been here before us." He turned around, flashing light into my face. "You?"

"How would I know about this when you just found out?"

He swung the flash back toward the pit. I struck a match to light a smoke. He jumped like he'd been stung. His flashlight went about. Then he made a choking sound and pointed.

I looked. A pink rosette was lying at the foot of the steps. It was one of the frills from Emily's flossy nightgown. It had torn off while we were pawing each other in panic. I cracked off, "All right, your girl friend is running this show."

"You—damn it—how do you know—?"

The man went wild. He swung at me with the flash and howled, "Damn you, you're part of a conspiracy to keep me from Diane! You and that—"

He had missed braining me, but the flash smashed on my shoulder. Then he piled in with fists, there in the stinking dark. The smell was awful now; not sea stench, but corpse odor. The dead were crying in the only way they could.

He slugged me a honey. Lucky he couldn't see what he was doing. I popped him one, heard him grunt.

"You damn fool, I'm not in cahoots with Emily; she's tricking them down into this den!"

But he wouldn't listen. He was off his chump. He growled and came back at me. I smashed against the wall. I'm not sure I could

*I said, "It's all right. If you're a prisoner, maybe I can help you."*

have swapped punches with him by daylight, but here it was impossible.

He was yelling like crazy now, and the echoes made it worse. Every lunge, he promised to kill me. I was sure now that Emily had tried to make him get rid of Diane; he figured that if I knew so much about the dame's nightgown, we had teamed up against him.

Every so often he connected and slugged me dizzy. Then I

ducked him and began bicycling, but there was nowhere to go. I saw a small flash of daylight overhead. There was an opening I'd naturally not seen when Emily took me down to the pit by night. I began to get the picture now. Some girl was leading the yokels along the cliff, and they'd stumble through and down into this stinking cave.

I yelled at him and pointed, but he wouldn't listen. He bored in toward the sound. There was a spattering of glass. He tripped on the lantern. Just then I got in a good wallop.

That and the damp paving did it. There was a thump, and he stopped yelling. Then I heard the soggy splash.

I struck a match. I was shaking all over. I was ready to park my fritters. Then a woman screeched, "So you did tell him! So you did drive him mad, ohhh—"

By the light of the match I saw it was Emily. She had a pistol in one hand and my flashlight in the other.

"Go down after him! Go down and tell him the villagers are going to finish the blonde witch—he was mine, he would have been—I belonged here, she didn't—go—go or I'll shoot you—"

Emily must have heard me yelling at Treganneth. She knew I had spilled the beans; that if I got loose, she was on the spot.

*THE* light blazed full in my eyes. I backed up a step. She laughed. The back of my legs was against the coping. I couldn't see the gun. I couldn't see a thing. I went wild like everyone else and made a dive to catch her around the knees.

She cut loose with the pistol, and she missed. Another shot, just as I stumbled and did get her about the knees. Before I could grab the gun, we toppled in a heap.

Behind me, a woman screamed: a woman with a lamp. The lamp spattered on the stones, and the flashlight rolled clear. There was a tangle of legs and feet and I couldn't get up. Two dames were mixing it.

One had bare legs. I tangled with a blanket shed in the show. The bare legs and the silk legs stumbled clear of me, and the flashlight, though I could see a white shape in the indirect glow. Diane and Emily toppled to the coping.

"Hold it!" I yelled, and kicked clear of the blanket.

I lunged, but I didn't grab Diane in time. Emily went over the side. There wasn't a thump this time; just a scream, the most horrible thing I'd ever heard. I pulled Diane away from the coping.

She was hysterical and couldn't say anything. I threw the blanket around her and reached for the flashlight lying on the floor. The switch lock disengaged, and I was shaking too much to make it stick again. Diane was saying, "Something happened to the lock; the door opened by itself. I slipped out to steal some of her clothes, and I saw her sneaking down with a gun. So I followed her."

Then she hung on tight and asked me what had happened. We were too shaky to crawl up the stairs. No sound came up from the pit.

I said we were too weak to move.

That's what I thought until a gleaming gray haze came up out of the dark: that dragon head with the long spike in the forehead, those terrific coils. Treganneth was kicking and threshing in one loop of the monster; there were other men in other coils. But that was pretty compared to what was on the unicorn spike.

Emily was speared clean through. The gleaming horn came out just below her breast. She was clawing, but there was no sound: just that apparition rising, with her draped over its forehead. Only the spike kept her from slipping off. But where the point touched the ceiling of the vault, the living smoke began to fade.

I said we were too sick to move, but when that thing began to thin out, I let out a yell and headed up the stairs, Diane and blanket included. Lucky she was hanging on. I wasn't going back for anything.

I stumbled into daylight. Diane slid from my arms and steadied herself against my shoulder. We both shook our heads. "Baby, that didn't happen. Don't ever tell anyone it did. Come on—"

I picked the lock of Emily's room and said, "Get some clothes. I'll hunt the car keys."

Diane grabbed my hand. "You stay right here. Even if you turned your back, I'd not be alone in this awful place."

I turned my back all right. The joke was on Diane. She was too shaken to notice the mirror angle. But that's not the payoff; that came after I'd bundled Diane into the old car and told the cops all about everything except the phantom monster.

The whole village was turned inside out. From that, and from searching the castle, especially Emily's room, we got the story. Treganneth's brother and Emily's husband had quarreled about her, and the two had finished each other. There were letters from yokels promising they'd kill her if she quit them to team up with the new lord. As I said, women were scarce, and she'd been a widow for seven years, and the village boys liked her.

So she started getting rid of her lovers, powdering her hair gilt to make Diane, the witch in the tower, take the rap when the lid blew off. With enough disappearances, something was bound to happen.

We had this all doped out when we went down into that vault. Then we looked over the edge. And that, I say, was the payoff.

There was a skeleton, a monstrous thing, in the pit. Some of the bones were still joined, though most were scattered on a ledge, or sunk in the slime. When the tide was low, the dead reeked in the mud; at high tide, the water blanketed them. Now it was low tide, and awful.

Treganneth was there, and so were the yokels. There were old skeletons, Treganneth's brother and Polgate, the steward who had kicked about a lord playing with Emily.

And Emily was there, speared on the horn that reached from the skull of the monoceros. There had been such a creature. That skull was what kept me from saying I must have been hypnotized.

I had seen the ghost of a monster god that men had worshiped before King Arthur came to town; worshiped by Druids, worshiped by the ancestors of a woman who played for a lord and lost. Now she belonged to a dead god. If it hadn't been for that skull, I'd never have *known* that I had seen the ghost of a god, of his victims.

Maybe that's why Diane and I stuck together when it was all over. It's kind of fun telling each other we did see it, that we weren't wacky.

# FLOWERS OF DESIRE

*It all sounded insane, this tale of the mysterious*
*cavern and the beautiful temptress. "There can*
*be but one mummy, and the mummy lives forever*
*with Her!" Were these the words of a crazy man,*
*or did they give the reason why he wanted to*
*carve himself a niche in the Vault of the Dead?*

"*H*ER BODY was like living alabaster. Her breasts were snowy, pearly globes. Her lips promised heaven… and her eyes warned of hell! And then… the dead men. Wrinkled old men, shriveled and dried and dead. Row after row of them in that underground place. *She* was the cause of it! Old men, wrinkled shriveled and dead…"

John Chamberlain's voice was flat and lifeless, like that of a child speaking an oft-rehearsed piece. He seemed totally oblivious to my presence—yet I was the cause of his talking. Which is to say that there was nobody else in the room with us. Just Chamberlain and myself. Yet, in effect, John Chamberlain ignored me. His droning monotone seemed more for his own ears than for mine.

He hesitated. Then: "Wrinkled and shriveled and dead! Wrinkled and shriveled and dead!" he repeated the phrase like a phonograph whose needle goes again and again interminably over the same groove.

"And you—?" I prompted.

"Yes, I? Oh, yes, I! There were but three of us alive and breathing in that cavern of horror. Spenser and the Mummy and I. And even now, Spenser—!" He shuddered; but I thought I detected a fascinated and yet terrified gleam in his half-closed eyes as he mentioned Spenser, the man with whom he had started out, five months before, on an archaeological expedition in the remote fastnesses of Central America.

"What of Spenser?" I persisted. It appeared almost impossible to break through John Chamberlain's subconscious mental barriers, to destroy the psychic armor in which he had clothed his soul. Yet I knew I had to bring him out of himself, compel him to give cohesion and unity to his wandering thoughts. It occurred to me that I would earn every cent his family had offered me to make him talk, to make some sense of his maunderings. "What of Spenser?" I queried him again, gently.

"Spenser? Ah, Spenser! He's still there—with *Her!* Making love to her! Holding her in his arms! Kissing her lips, caressing her. He… *took the Mummy's place!*"

*I COULD* not pretend to understand this. I had been warned to expect some such vague statement. But—was this vague or senseless enough to warrant committing an otherwise sound man to an asylum for the balance of his natural life? As an alienist and psychiatrist, I did not think so. Moreover, I was intrigued by the mystery of Spenser's disappearance. Spenser had been John Chamberlain's partner on that expedition. Chamberlain had returned. Spenser had not.

What, then, had become of Spenser?

Only Chamberlain could reveal the answer—and Chamberlain's mind wandered on the borderland of madness. Again he said: "Spenser took the Mummy's place…!"

"What mummy?" I pursued.

"The *Mummy!*" Chamberlain exclaimed peevishly. "The only living thing Spenser and I had found in that cave of death and silence and passion!"

"But how could Spenser have taken the mummy's place?"

"Because Spenser wished to live… forever… with *Her!*"

This was utter madness, I perceived. Yet I pretended to comprehend that which was inexplicable. "I see," I murmured. "But why—why didn't you, too, stay on? Why didn't you remain with Spenser? Why did you return to civilization?"

"Because there can be but one *Mummy*. And the flowers, the blossoms… they nauseated me. Their odor, their fragrance, their perfume—like a drug! I felt sick. I couldn't stay. And… I was jealous! Spenser had *Her!* For his own! Her lips, her golden hair, she belonged to Spenser as long as he would live. As long as he drew breath, she could never be mine…"

*HERE* seemed to be a tiny ray of light through Chamberlain's dark brain cloud. But even as he uttered his jealousy of Spenser, a mask-like sullenness settled over his haggard features. He subsided into moody silence, like a man sinking into some morass of soundless evil.

Intuitively I realized that this mysterious *"She"* whom he had mentioned was a subject either delicate or sore; one that seemed effectively to dam his uneven, halting flow of speech.

Again I shifted my approach.

"How had you and Spenser found the cave?" I strove to affect an air of casual inquiry.

"We had passed through the jungle. There was a clearing. The

*"We seemed to be traveling a level pathway, when of a sudden we saw her—the Queen of the Dead!"*

ground was high, like a plateau—a mesa. That same night our native bearers and guides deserted us. We attributed the desertion to some sort of local superstition—a tribal tabu. Our head guide had warned us the place was bewitched. We had laughed. Especially Spenser. How he had laughed! We were fools, both of us. Fools, fools, fools! Row after row of dead men... wrinkled and old and withered. Dried and wrinkled and withered and dead..."

He trailed off into somber silence.

"You climbed this plateau, you and Spenser?"

"Yes. Alone. Our supplies cached under a cairn. Spenser led the way. He sang. He always sang! I wonder... if he's singing now...!" Chamberlain laughed shortly, unmusically, gratingly.

"Then Spenser still lives?"

"Lives? He will live forever—in *Her* arms! Or until...."

"Until what?"

"Until another fool takes the Mummy's place!"

"You mean—?"

"Spenser is the Mummy!"

"But I thought you said there were three of you in the cave. Spenser, and the Mummy, and yourself?"

"Yes. So there were. But that was only at first."

"When you first came upon the cave?"

"Yes. That's it. There was a rolling rise on the plateau—like a woman's breast. We approached it, Spenser and I. It looked nearer than it actually was. It was dusk of the second day when we finally came to its base. Then we rested. Under the stars. The stars shine brightly there."

Chamberlain seemed not to see me, not to see the four walls of the room where his family had kept him virtually a prisoner these past three weeks since his return from Central America. He seemed to be looking beyond—into the dim jungles and up toward the tropic stars.

*I WAITED* for him to continue. I felt queerly alone in my responsibility. Upon my diagnosis would rest Chamberlain's freedom—or his lifelong incarceration in some institution for the insane.

"We slept," he resumed at last. "It must have been midnight when Spenser awakened me. He shook me gently. "There is someone here!" he whispered.

"Then what happened?"

"When Spenser awakened me and told me someone was near us, I raised up. It was moonlight. I saw a shadow moving—heard a stealthy footstep in the dried grass.

"Spenser and I sprang to our feet. A man stood before us. In the moon glow we saw him. A man. No, not a man. A *Mummy!*"

"From the rows of the dead?" I ventured. It was mad, monstrous, this tale.

"No. Not yet. This Mummy was alive—alive with the dead life of centuries."

Such a paradox was insanity, of course. But I led Chamberlain on. "And then—?"

"The Mummy was unafraid. Spenser and I perceived that he meant us no harm. He beckoned to us, and we followed. I didn't want to follow him, yet a weird hypnotic magnet seemed to be drawing me onward.

"There was an aperture, an orifice, in the rolling breast of land. The Mummy scuttled into it, slithering across the dried grass. He was practically naked. His skin was like wrinkled and withered parchment. He beckoned for us to enter the cave after him.

"The breast was hollow inside, like a dead crater of some extinct volcano. There was a crystal pool at its center. Bottomless, we learned afterward.

"The Mummy skirted the pool. Still we trailed behind him. Then, suddenly, the Mummy disappeared!"

"A ghost, then?" I asked.

Chamberlain shot me a quick, curious, sidelong glance. "No. The Mummy was not a ghost. He had merely entered a cavern."

"This cavern opened from the inside of the extinct crater?"

"Yes. Spenser and I peered in. Again the Mummy beckoned us. But it was dark—and the moon was nearly down. So we shook our heads. Then the Mummy turned and left us. We heard him padding and slithering into the bowels of the cave. And that was all."

"YOU'RE sure this wasn't all a dream, Chamberlain?" I asked him softly.

He looked at me. His next words startled me so that I jumped a little. "You, too, think I'm mad, don't you, doctor?" he inquired cannily.

"Why, Mr. Chamberlain, I—" I floundered.

He smiled wanly. "I know. Don't apologize. Perhaps I am a little mad. It's the perfume of those flowers always in my nostrils—and the beauty of *Her* features and *Her* body constantly before my eyes. And those rows of dead men… old… and wrinkled… and withered…"

The clouds again! They drifted in, obscuring the smile from Chamberlain's face, smothering the flicker of sanity in his eyes, stifling his mind in little gusts and eddies.

"You and Spenser stayed outside the cave all that night?" I prompted him.

"Yes. Spenser and I stood watch-and-watch until dawn. And when the rising sun at last shimmered down on the crystal pool, the Mummy reappeared from the cave.

"Once more he gestured for us to enter with him. There was light in the cave now—we could see it trickling in like volatile liquid through interstices in the cavern's roof.

"Spenser laughed. He was always laughing and singing! And he followed the Mummy, like the brave fool he was. I took a last look at the rising sun... and then... God help me... I went on into the cave behind Spenser and the Mummy!

"The cave did not seem to have much downward pitch except as it conformed to the convolutions of the roof, which was the rolling breast of land. Along the way the sunlight trickled in like molten gold—yet I had the sensation of burrowing deep down in the earth's bowels.

"At once we were in a room—a great bare hall chiseled out of living rock. It was circular—perfectly circular. Cunning hands had wrought that space. It was the Court of the Dead—the old ones... the wrinkled ones... the withered ones..."

I tried to keep him from going back to that monotonous mumble. "You saw them there? The dead men?"

"*HOW* could I fail? Rows upon rows of them, each peacefully reclining in his niche along the walls! Row after row of dead men, wrinkled men, withered old men... sleeping the sleep of countless centuries in little hollowed rock apertures, like the bunks of a ship. Mummies, all! Naked. Their skins like desiccated parchment. Replicas in dead flesh of the living Mummy who led us onward. Niches around the entire circle. From the level of the floor to the vaulted ceiling. They were at peace; some seemed to be faintly smiling.

"Spenser and I were led to the opposite side of the vault. There was another passage leading from it. I noticed that on either side of this far entrance there were no mummies, no niches... but no! I looked again. There was one new niche, not yet completely hollowed out. In it were crude drilling tools. Someone was preparing another resting place for a new member of this company of dead, silent guardians...

"And there was the faint trace of an odor, a fragrance—sweet, full, heavy, like a combined lily and tuberose and magnolia. Like the scent of a flower never before grown on earth.

"I hung back, suddenly afraid. But Spenser only laughed. His laughter jarred strangely in that silent place of the dead. He laughed again, and sang a snatch of song. I felt ashamed of my own timidity. I could not let myself be known as a coward when Spenser was so brave. Then the Mummy led us from the vault, into that passageway on the far side.

"Now we seemed to be traveling a level pathway. And then... suddenly we saw... *Her!*"

Chamberlain stopped. Pain shot across his features as if at a memory he would have preferred to allow to remain dormant.

"You saw Her," I urged him. "Did she approach you?"

"No. To the contrary, we approached *Her*. The Queen of the Dead."

**BEADS** of perspiration stood out on Chamberlain's forehead. His hands shook. "She lay there on an upraised dais of hewn rock. God, how can I describe her unearthly, heavenly, hellish beauty? She was nude except for a jeweled girdle about her white loins. Her graceful white arms were folded across her flat stomach. Her breasts were sheer perfection—perfectly moulded.

Her features were so beautiful that the mind reeled and staggered to behold them. Her hair—I cannot describe its color; it was as if God or Satan had crowned her with an aureole, a halo of loveliness tinted with a brush dipped in the palette of the Infinite. Not brown. Not gold. The color of a shimmering mountain in the setting sun!

"Her skin had the appearance, the texture, of creamy ivory. Not milk-white, nor yet was it the pallor of death. But there was not the faintest trace of a blush of color to mar the pallid evenness of her satin-marble flesh. Her eyes were closed, and her smiling lips were red—brilliant, vivid red. Startling! The lower lip was faintly open; I could see the gleam of her tiny white teeth…"

"She slept?" I ventured softly, afraid to intrude and perhaps shatter the spell of his returning memory.

"Yes. She slept… as She had been sleeping… for centuries! Since the first of that dead company in the outer vault had held Her in his arms for the last time, kissed Her… and then lain down

*"—There was the mummy—
the only living thing we found
in this cavern of horror!"*

forever in the first niche which he had hewn for himself in the circular chamber."

"You say she slept, Chamberlain. But what of the perfume, the fragrance?"

"It rose in heady waves from a circle of strange and curious white blossoms that grew in a single row from a fissure in the rocky floor of this inner cave. The fissure encircled and enclosed the stony couch upon which lay the Queen of the Dead. The strange flowers guarded Her body.

"I watched, at first, with an odd sense of dreadful awe, for Her breathing. I wanted to see the faint stirring of her beautiful breasts. Days passed before I could bring myself to realize that She would never breathe. And all around her grew those encircling flowers— as if to pour forth their anaesthetic perfume to overcome any who might wish to defile with human touch that beautiful, enchanted, dead Queen. They were Her bodyguard, those blossoms. Guardians of Her lovely body…!"

"After you first saw her, what happened?" I asked.

CHAMBERLAIN'S eyes grew dreamy. "Spenser no longer laughed. No longer sang. His voice was hushed. Together, he and I stood in numbed silence, reeling with Her beauty, drunken with the heavy, intoxicating perfume of Her flowers.

"The Mummy beckoned for us to follow him out of Her chamber. He started out the way we had entered. Then madness seemed to overpower Spenser. 'No!' he cried. 'No! I'll not leave!' And he started toward Her, as if to lift her and take her in his arms…

"But something in the Mummy's warning gesture—something spell-like, eerie, stopped Spenser in his tracks. The Mummy shook his withered head. What was his evil power over us? Spenser and I stood frozen, hypnotized. We saw the Mummy pluck one of those blossoms. Even as he plucked it… *another flower burgeoned and bloomed on the ravished stem!* A flower to replace the one which the Mummy had taken…

"Then the Mummy inhaled deeply of the blossom he had plucked. Something happened to him. A queer, monstrous impossibility. His shriveled skin lost its dry texture. His flesh seemed to swell and become normal before our very eyes. His sinews flexed. As Spenser and I watched in terror, he became another creature. He was transformed. It was a miracle. He was no longer a Mummy. *He was a man!* A superb, muscular, virile man!

"He had been rejuvenated and made young by the fragrance of that hell-damned blossom!

"And now he approached *Her*. He took her in his arms. He kissed her crimson, still lips. With her in his embrace, he became the very epitome of loving virility. Shamelessly, there while Spenser and I watched in the thralls of a hypnosis that fettered out muscles and our voices, he made love to her."

"And did she respond?" I asked quietly.

"She was like lifeless clay, unresponsive, limp, dead. Yet somehow I seemed to have the impression that she was not dead to that other man—the man who held her in his arms. The man who a moment before had been a shriveled, living mummy. To him, She had life and fire and passion. Intuitively I knew that; and Spenser knew it, also.

"Then at last, when the man had tired, he arranged Her once more upon her dais of hewn rock. Her eyes were still closed; her red lips still smiled faintly. And when it was over, Spenser grabbed my arm. His fingers bit into my flesh. 'Look!' he whispered.

"My blood congealed in my veins. Even as I watched, that unknown man was turning back into a dried, desiccated, living mummy! Only now, as the transformation took place, he seemed even more wrinkled and old and shriveled than before.

"The Mummy beckoned to Spenser and to me. This time we followed him without question. We followed him from Her black, enchanted chapel as meekly as slaves."

"The Mummy led you and Spenser from the cavern?" I asked.

"Yes. Through the passageway and into the circular Court of the Dead. Thence up into the sunlight he conducted us. We saw the sun, and I stiffened in amazement. It was setting! In the short, fleeting space of a few moments, a day had passed!"

I nodded understanding.

*JOHN CHAMBERLAIN* continued wearily. "Spenser and I slept in the open that night—the last night for many to come. The last night forever for Spenser. Lucky Spenser! Damn him…!"

I whispered: "And what of the Mummy?"

"He remained silent, as he had always been. Wordless. He conducted us into the open. By signs he bade us wash and drink at the crystal pool. I felt giddy from hunger; yet when I had drunk from those bottomless, sparkling waters I found that my appetite had vanished. It was as if I had consumed both food and drink. Sleep overtook Spenser and me immediately after that. We seemed drugged. We slumbered under the far, bright stars.

"The next morning, the Mummy awakened us. He led us once more into the cave. But at the great circular Vault of the Dead he stopped us. Spenser wanted to press onward to Her chamber; but the Mummy shook his head.

"And then for three days we stayed there in that great round vault, never leaving for food or drink; never moving save when night fell and we stretched in dreamless slumber among those others who slept so well… We stretched on the great vault's floor with dead men on every side of us and the Mummy, a living cadaver, for company.

"Daily we watched, fascinated, while the Mummy hewed at that new niche in the wall. It dawned upon us—some sort of weird telepathy, perhaps, for the Mummy never spoke—that he hewed it for himself!

"Gradually the history of that Cave of the Dead seemed to seep into my inner consciousness as it must have reached Spencer's. Each of these dead, withered, wrinkled men had been a guardian… and a lover… to that beautiful, sleeping dead Queen in the other room! Each had remained a silent votary at the shrine of her still, unearthly beauty, with his days occupied in the hewing of a niche that he himself would some day occupy when his successor appeared.

"And now—either Spenser or I had been selected as the present Mummy's successor! One of us would take up that silent, sinister guardianship after the present Mummy, with his labors completed, settled himself in his newly-hewn niche to sleep the last long dreamless sleep.

"Dreamless? I cannot believe the Mummy thought that!" Chamberlain added as an afterthought.

"Why not?" I asked him.

"Because the Mummy loved *Her*. He would not have willingly relinquished her to someone else unless he thought he would possess her in his death dreams! Remember, during all the years he had been in this cave he had been her lover... Whenever he plucked one of those hell-spawned flowers that surrounded her bier!"

**CHAMBERLAIN** smiled wryly. "Strange, perhaps, that two educated men like Spenser and myself—world-traveled, sophisticated—should have fallen under the queer spell of that hellish place! Yet neither of us thought it so when our minds turned toward the ultimate day when one or the other of us would be chosen to take the Mummy's place.

"Then I noticed that Spenser was growing restive. It seemed that a powerful magnet were drawing him inexorably toward that inner sanctuary where She lay in regally simple state. He was commencing to chafe at the restraint which the Mummy placed on him.

"But on the morning of the fourth day, everything ended. The Mummy had finished his last resting place!

"We watched, fascinated, as he quietly put down his cutting tools. He turned to us and beckoned. He led us toward the passage that gave entrance to Her silent chamber.

"A freakish, hellish fear suddenly laid hold of us. Worms of dread ate into my mind, crawled through my cringing flesh. Something snapped within my being, and stark terror flooded my very veins. I turned and ran the other way—out, out into the warm sunlight which I had not seen in four days except as it filtered through fissures in the cavern's roof.

"But Spenser was not the coward I was. He followed the Mummy, a smile at his lips..."

I looked at John Chamberlain. "You never saw Spenser again?"

*"I picked up the blossoms that had given me my glimpse of her as a living woman—and suddenly I saw three white maggots in the heart of the flower!"*

"Wait. I have not finished the tale. All that day I waited outside the mouth of the cave. I was filled with inexplicable, suppurating fear. I was frightened at the prospect of being alone; afraid to venture back into the cave to search for Spenser; filled with a strange dread of something I could not name.

"Night fell. I could not sleep. I crept to the crystal pool, bathed my fevered face, drank deep of the cool waters. And then... I slept...

"*PERHAPS* it was the next morning; perhaps it was weeks later. I cannot tell. But the sun was high when I wakened at last.

"Spenser stood over me. In horror I stared at him—at the change the cave had wrought in his appearance. He was wrinkled and old and withered. Before he spoke, I knew that the Mummy was… dead. And now… *Spenser was the Mummy!*"

Chamberlain shuddered.

"Yes. Go on," I urged him softly.

He drew a deep, quivering breath. "Spenser spoke to me, but his voice seemed thick and croaking, his tongue thick from long disuse. His clothing was falling from him. He seemed shrunken. His skin had the appearance of new parchment. But when he smiled, it was the ghost of his old carefree smile.

" 'She's come to life, Chamberlain!' he exulted over me hoarsely. 'She's mine! I've broken the spell—the spell of enchantment! I've plucked the flowers of desire that surround her, and their fragrance brought her to life! She's mine, I tell you! I've kissed her lips and thrilled to her warmth and felt her arms about my neck…! I have become… her lover…!'

"I stared at Spenser. 'You mean you've…?'

" 'Yes! And the courtiers—they've risen to serve us! I'm in Paradise, Chamberlain! Paradise!' And his eyes gleamed glass-like as he slithered and scuttled toward the crystal pool to drink his fill.

"There was something wrong with Spenser. I knew it. I grew afraid of him—deathly afraid. I tried to talk to him, to reason with him, to make him realize and understand that he was insane when he believed that She could come to life with him there in that hellish cavern of perfumed horror. I tried to make him understand that he was drugged—drugged by the scent of those Satanic blossoms.

"But he only laughed at me—a madman's cackling laugh. A mummy's rustling laugh! Around him I detected the heady, heavy scent of Her flowers. Flowers of enchantment. Flowers of desire. And with a wave of his hand, as if to taunt me, Spenser went back into the cave.

"I followed him, silently, hoping to seize him and overpower him and drag him back to sanity by force, if necessary. I planned to knock him unconscious, bind him, get him back to civilization with me."

"You followed him, Chamberlain?" I whispered. My own palms were strangely moist.

"Yes. Followed him into the cave. Spenser was not in the circular Vault of the Dead when I reached it. But I saw that latest niche—and there was a figure in it. The figure of the Mummy who had first led us into that place of evil. That Mummy was dead now, just as I had expected. Then I saw something else that brought a shudder to my spine. A new niche was being hollowed in the wall. Understanding came to me. Spenser was hollowing that new niche... for himself...

"*MY* terror knew no bounds; but my friendship for Spenser was greater than my fear. So I went down that far passage toward Her sanctuary. I knew Spenser would be there... with Her...

"And there I found him. He had plucked one of the blossoms that grew about her bier. He had inhaled its deadly fragrance and cast it aside, while a new bloom burgeoned to replace the flower that had been plucked.

"Spenser had inhaled that poisonous-sweet perfume. And now he was himself again, physically. He no longer possessed the outward appearance of a mummy. He was strong, masculine... and he was taking Her up in his arms. I saw his eyes, and they were the dead eyes of a madman.

"As if transfixed, I watched. I saw Spenser kiss Her on the lips, eagerly, ardently, as if he could never have enough. I saw his hands on her shoulders and her hips and her white, beautifully rounded waist. He... was like a beast made wild by desire....

"I sprang at him, pulled him away from Her. He whirled, saw me, fought me like an uncaged tiger. But somehow I managed to hit him on the jaw. He fell at my feet, unconscious and gasping. And as he fell, I saw his muscles shrivel and wither. I saw his skin change and lose color. He became... a Mummy...!

"I leaned over him to pick him up and carry him out of the

cave. But he had fallen near the discarded blossom he had plucked. Somehow, I inhaled of its deadly, enchanting fragrance. I felt a sudden volatile sensation coursing through my veins and into my soul. It was like an overwhelming burst of passionate frenzy…

"I dropped Spenser and turned to the bier on which She lay. And then—Oh, God!—*I saw her open her eyes and smile at me!*

"She held out her white arms, lazily, invitingly… even as I had a sudden raging desire to hold her in my arms, crush her against me. I started toward her. She would be mine!

"Then somehow my vision seemed blurred. It seemed that She was once more lying straight and still and lifeless on her bier. Then I realized that there was only one way in which I could ever see her… as a living, breathing being…"

"Only one way, Chamberlain?"

"**YES.** I must inhale the fragrance of Her flowers! The perfume would drug me and make Her seem to be alive! Swiftly I turned, and picked up the blossom which Spenser had plucked. The blossom I had smelled when I leaned over him. The blossom that had given me my first glimpse of Her as a moving, living being. I picked up the flower, held it before my face. And then—oh, God in heaven—

*"And then I saw three fat white crawling maggots squirming in the heart of the flower!* Maggots… such as might fester in a decomposed corpse!

"With an oath I flung the cancerous blossom from me. The enchantment, the spell, was broken. The scales had fallen from my eyes. I saw Her, now, as someone long dead… a corpse… a dead thing out of hell's slimy jaws!

"Staggering, I went to Spenser, lifted him, carried him out of Her sanctuary. In the sweetish, fetid perfume that battered at my senses I fought myself onward, with Spenser lying limp in my arms. Wave after wave of revulsion struck at my stomach, made me desire to retch. I was nearly overwhelmed by that demoniac fragrance before I could get Spenser out of that inner cavern.

"I carried him through the circular Vault of the Dead; and at last I had him out in the warm sun of noontide. I brought him to the brink of the crystal pool; I bathed his face in the waters, forced a little into his mouth, chafed his parchment wrists. I begged, implored him to open his eyes and listen to me.

"Finally he awakened. His gaze fell upon me with surprise and with a terrible anger. He was conscious, but he was too weak to resist my efforts. Yet he could hear what I was saying.

" 'Spenser!' I cried. 'For God's sake, Spenser, come to yourself! You realize what's happening! You're drugging yourself with those hellish flowers! You're going mad! You're steeping yourself in that fragrance out of hell, and in your delirium you're imagining that She has come to life! But it's false! False, I tell you! It's all a drunken, drugged fantasy! You'll stay here and rot and dry up and wither… with your drug-dreams for company! And a niche in that cave when it all ends!

" 'Spenser… throw off this spell of black sorcery! Those people in there are mummies, not men and a woman! It's the chemical action of the air in the cave that has preserved them through the centuries. Wake up, Spenser… come away with me! Leave those corpses to rot in hell where they belong!'

"I didn't realize how quickly Spenser was regaining his strength. It must have been the water from the pool which I had forced past his lips. Suddenly he jumped to his feet and struck me a great blow with his fist so that I fell to the ground. 'Damn you, Chamberlain, keep your jealously to yourself!' he snarled. 'Dreams or reality… what does it matter as long as I have Her? And I shall have Her as long as I live! I shall kiss her lips!… forever! Forever, you hear me, Chamberlain? Forever, until someone comes to replace me!

" 'Now go, damn you, before I kill you and throw you into the pool!' Then he slithered back into the cave and disappeared into the blackness while I still screamed and mouthed pleas for him to throw off the curse of those drugged flowers of desire….

"But he never came out of the cave again, and I was afraid to go in after him. Afraid that I might inhale the fragrance of those blossoms and become as Spenser was. A Mummy…."

"So you left Spenser there, Chamberlain?"

"Yes. He's still there… a *Mummy* now… withered and wrinkled and old... patiently hewing out his niche where some day he'll lie dead. But meanwhile... each night he holds Her in his arms...."

"While you...?"

"While I," Chamberlain finished bitterly, "have returned to civilization... and to emptiness! Always the vision of Her face before my eyes! Always the odor of those enchanted blossoms in my nostrils! And... always my consuming desire to touch Her and kiss Her lips surrounded by those mummies... wrinkled and withered and shriveled and dead..." His voice faded into that flat monotone of madness.

*I PRONOUNCED* John Chamberlain sane but suffering from a highly nervous condition, and I recommended a year of rest at some private sanitarium. He accepted my dictum willingly enough, although at first his family protested that he should be confined for life in an asylum for the hopelessly deranged.

So Chamberlain went to a sanitarium. But a month later he vanished, taking with him a considerable sum of money which he withdrew from his account on the pretext of purchasing a country estate of his own where he might rest undisturbed. He never bought such a place; he disappeared. Those close to him are under the impression that in a sudden spell of madness he committed suicide; but I alone know otherwise. I had a brief note from him:

> *"My dear Dr. :*
> *Thanks for your patience and understanding. You are the only one who knows the true story. I never repeated it to anyone else. Now I find I cannot stand to be any longer away from Her. Spenser has had his fling. He probably won't even recognize me when I appear at the cave. If he does... well, he's only a Mummy now, and I can handle him. I'm going to hew a niche for myself in the Vault of the Dead... I'm going to steep myself in the perfume of the Flowers of Desire... and I'm going to hold Her in my arms... forever....*
> *Yours,*
> *John Chamberlain."*

www.ingramcontent.com/pod-product-compliance
Lightning Source LLC
Chambersburg PA
CBHW051821020726
47502CB00005B/1562